The Scent of a Lie

The Scent
of a Lie

paulo da costa

**A RIVERRUN
NEW FICTION BOOK**

Ekstasis Editions

National Library of Canada Cataloguing in Publication Data

Da Costa, Paulo.
 The scent of a lie

 ISBN 1-894800-07-9

 I. Title.
 PS8557.A24S33 2002   C813'.6   C2002-910331-2
 PR9199.4.D22S33 2002

Published in 2002 by:
Ekstasis Editions Canada Ltd.   Ekstasis Editions
Box 8474, Main Postal Outlet   Box 571
Victoria, B.C. V8W 3S1   Banff, Alberta ToL oCo

THE CANADA COUNCIL | LE CONSEIL DES ARTS
   FOR THE ARTS | DU CANADA
    SINCE 1957 | DEPUIS 1957

BRITISH   *The*
COLUMBIA
ARTS COUNCIL
Supported by the Province of British Columbia

Scent of a Lie has been published with the assistance of a grant from the Canada Council for the Arts and the British Columbia Arts Council through Cultural Services Branch of British Columbia.

Contents

The Scent of a Lie

Roses for the Dead

Padre Lucas found rest under an olive tree. He pressed his hand-kerchief to the halo of white hair around his skull, attempting to suppress the beaded sweat drenching his face. He leaned against the olive trunk, contemplating the green quilt covering the valley floor, tracing the corn patches and grape fields stitched together by a thread of stone hedges. The sinuous River Caima, unusually brilliant under the sun, forced him to squint. He shielded his face. The river, the earth's open artery, crossed the heart of the valley, delivering life and fertility to the fields. Intricate veins burst from the main artery, channelling precious water to remote places along the hillside.

From the vantage point on the hill crest, Padre Lucas relished the angels' vista across Vale D'Água Amargurada. In the distance, his destination, the Mateus mansion, was but a crumb engulfed by a swarm of ants.

The noon sun and the slope scant of trees had arrested his progress. He perspired inside the black cassock. His chest rose and sank in futile attempts to expel the burning air. His nostrils flared and puffed from exertion. Padre Lucas was a sight matched only by strained bulls pulling logs up the incline. He now clasped a rosary in the infernal heat and muttered a string of curses under his breath. Parishioners he encountered on the dusty trail asked him to add their intentions to his prayers.

Half a century ago Padre Lucas had arrived with a wooden crucifix dangling from his neck and an immaculate Bible in hand, eager to guard his assigned flock of parishioners. Fresh from the seminary, words of justice and compassion had leaped easily from his mouth. Short lived words, words lasting as long as trout baited out of the River Caima. An earnest crowd of peasants had awaited him while a child timidly stepped forward and placed a bouquet of red roses in his hands. A reception of Senhores, led by Ambrósio Mateus, ceremoniously welcomed him.

"It's the honourable Senhores' pleasure to present you with the key to the newly built parish house. Maria will be at your service, overseeing your domestic matters. Nothing fancy. Adequate for a soul like yours, only concerned with matters of the Spirit and the Heavens. The day to day business of earthly matters, we will attend to," Ambrósio declared as the Senhores clapped.

The Senhores informed him that everyone regretted the tragic accident that had befallen his predecessor, Padre Baptista. A hunting party of Senhores, tricked by the devilish dusk, had shot the unfortunate man, mistaking the priest for a lone black wolf.

"Terrible tragedy. If only we understood the Lord's ways, His will, calling home a disciple after only a year of service. A year of youthful misguided sermons on meaningless mortal matters, failing to give guidance to the people's spiritual hunger," Senhor Ambrósio said, placing his heavy hand on Padre Lucas' shoulder. Padre Lucas assented with a nod of his head and his fist tightened around the rose stems, thorns sinking into his flesh, drawing a trickle of blood. Padre Lucas watched peasants in the fields below him. He had grown accustomed to the sight of his peasant parishioners shaving the mountain face and carving precarious terraces up the hillside. From the crown of the hill where Padre Lucas sat, the fields resembled a stairway to heaven. It was as if the peasants were fleeing a hell pit, moving heavenwards, seeking a better life.

Padre Lucas mused on why his parishioners were flocking to the Mateus mansion for a last glance at the stern body of the man who had tyrannised their lives. Was it curiosity, the opportunity to tread upon their oppressor's varnished wooden floor, or witness to the end of his reign?

He observed the mourning crowd, a black human stain, spilling from the mansion, spreading quickly over the surrounding land.

As Padre Lucas walked solemnly to the mansion's stone portico, the sea of people parted.

A moat of tables lined the mansion's periphery, serving maize bread, salted olives and lupini beans, sweet breads and jams. The quince jam and the sweet breads attracted the peasants the way a sugar spill attracts a scurry of ants. A decent meal, at last.

To clothe the peasants eager to pay their last respects, proper attire waited at the entrance. Black veils, shawls and kerchiefs for the women. Black polished shoes, ties and suit jackets for the men. For most peasants, it was the first time they had walked in shoes. Their wobbly steps dragged the polished slickness of leather in a shuffle around the casket.

Padre Lucas entered the sombre living room and hesitated, feeling the blast of a thousand candles burn his face.

"May the Father of Mercies, the God of all consolation be with you," he greeted those present.

The stench of burnt paraffin assaulted his senses. He pinched his nose. Through the black haze of candle smoke, he recognised Senhor Ambrósio Mateus in his Sunday suit. The corpse lay nearly buried under red carnations. Carnations stolen from his garden and tossed into the coffin by the constant throng of peasants. Ambrósio's umbrella rested on his folded forearm. Throughout his life, rain or shine, Senhor Ambrósio had leaned on the umbrella's solid oak stump, as someone else might lean on an amicable shoulder. The umbrella, a loyal companion unto death.

Padre Lucas walked towards Senhor Ambrósio's grandson and successor, Mário, a young man weeping under the inherited burden of wealth and power. Padre Lucas voiced condolences, vigorously shook Mário's limp hand and remarked, "The souls of the just are in the hands of God, and no torment shall touch them." The Senhores from Vale D'Água Amargurada nodded in agreement. The peasants murmured.

The Senhores stood erect, arms crossed over their chests, surrounding Mário in a protective circle. A rose brightened each black suit, stem and thorns buried in their breast pockets.

Padre Lucas raised his hands, supplicating to God, and recited an opening prayer,

> "O God,
> to whom mercy and forgiveness belong,
> hear our prayers and command that Senhor Ambrósio
> be carried safely home to heaven
> and come to enjoy your eternal reward."

"Amen," replied those present.

Padre Lucas stood by Mário's side and patiently waited for the final trickle of people to pay their last respects.

Most peasants hurried past, not bothering a glance at the body, merely following the trajectory towards the food tables. Others genuflected, their mournful respects shed genuine tears of relief. Padre Lucas had tread upon the valley dirt long enough to have personal thoughts about God and the limitations of his compassionate teachings.

Senhor Ambrósio's corpse lay contemplating a wall covered with his own life-size portraits. There, he posed against a faded backdrop of exotic buildings—mosques, Padre Lucas guessed. The flickering flames painted a dancing, devilish glow over Ambrósio's shrewd smile.

On the celebrated occasion of Senhor Ambrósio's return to his birth village, the pretentious portraits had hung in the public square for everyone to admire. He had secretly posed in garments borrowed from the war museum and had paid starving artists to paint extravagant scenes of valour. Medals of courage dangled from his chest to support his constructed tales of gallantry and heroism. Other paintings, depicting the pillage of infidels as an endeavour blessed by God, were meant to command the valley's sympathy and absolve him of his sudden wealth and vast possessions.

Senhor Ambrósio's erratic confessions had shed scant light on the details of his life; but a repentance the previous night, during his Last Rites, had released the burden of Ambrósio's story to Padre Lucas. The final guardian of the events that had shaped his existence.

Relaxing from his church affairs, an urgent call for his services had interrupted Padre Lucas' customary *sesta*. Senhor Ambrósio Mateus, panicking at the prospect of dying unconfessed, promised Padre Lucas, in exchange for the expiation of his sins, the most beautiful cathedral ever built on the Iberian peninsula. This promise encouraged Padre Lucas' prompt attention to Senhor Ambrósio's soul and made the eulogy a somewhat easier task.

The last peasant shuffled past Padre Lucas. He opened the Bible,

"Lord, in our grief we turn to you.
Are you not the God of love
who opens your ears to all?…"

13

Padre Lucas knew what to voice on such occasions but pretended to follow the Book—citing a liturgy that invited Senhor Ambrósio to depart from his earthly dwelling and join Padre Lucas in the ceremonious steps, towards his last residence. There, he would join other good Christian souls in the Kingdom of God. Padre Lucas closed the Bible and sprinkled Holy Water on the body. The coffin's lid was sealed, the pall draped, and a miniature golden cross placed on top. As the four strongest men in the village raised it to their shoulders a handle collapsed and tipped the coffin sideways causing a great commotion. The coffin lid flew open.

Senhor Ambrósio had become a heavy man after decades of excess. His sausage fingers clasped his stomach bulge—a feast for the ants, Padre Lucas could not help thinking. Accordions of flesh rolled down his neck and compressed at the chin, giving the impression of three mouths.

Padre Lucas re-fashioned a perfect pose, folded Senhor Ambrósio's arms over his chest. A repenting pose for his farewell journey to eternity.

During his Last Rites, Senhor Ambrósio confessed to Padre Lucas that life had not always been bountiful. As a child he did not remember his stomach in any other state but one of perpetual growling and complaining. Sometimes the hollow rumble echoed through his bones and reached the ear of a passerby. It was an incessant chorus accompanied by the choreography of his begging, outstretched arm. A scrawny, rachitic bone stretching his skin, "Sir, Madam, for Christ's charity leave a morsel of bread."

At night on his return home, he would stop at the butcher's back door, wrestling discarded bones from the jaws of a stray dog, strings of flesh still attached, which he carried home to be softened into soup.

His peasant parents, landless and further debilitated by lung afflictions, had no Senhor to wage them. They were not worth exploiting. Faced with perishing misery, his father forced Ambrósio to crush his brother's infant legs with a rock. A healthy child, deformed to incite pity in the hearts of whomever laid eyes on him. A reminder to everyone, even the peasants, that there were worse fates than poverty. An appeal to their generosity. The sight of misfortune, his father said, brought compassion.

The peasants, possessing hardly a crumb to share, offered nothing but their tears. The Senhores, having their conscience temporarily smudged, "As if the world's tragedies were of our making, as if his crooked legs were our responsibility," scolded Ambrósio for the bad taste he exhibited, their idyllic afternoon promenade ruined.

Soon, the Senhores and their wives avoided the crossroads where Ambrósio and his brother were planted amid clouds of flies. Ambrósio, expressionless, stared at his brother's useless legs. He recalled the day his mother announced the pregnancy. He had wished for a brother to chase his soccer ball of rags. Staring at the crippled legs, Ambrósio knew that never again would he taste the saltiness of pain. His tears dammed up like a river, choking his spirit.

With the failure of his father's stratagem, Ambrósio escaped the valley to fend for his own life, finding a daily meal as a servant in an aristocratic mansion in Lisbon. Carrying his insatiable hunger and the nightmare of his brother, Ambrósio was determined to fill the emptiness that cursed his stomach and his life. Having learned that to survive he must be tougher than the rest, Ambrósio tackled life as a battle to be won or lost. He had tasted the loser's fate. He swore his heirs would never suffer from deprivation. His obsession with wealth callused his heart to indignities and humiliations. A humble start, a message boy, he was victim to the outbursts accompanying bad news, "Pray for good news boy and you'll earn a centavo. Three lashings otherwise," his master told him.

From the old butler, he learned to use a hot coal iron to soften the glue sealing the house correspondence. The old butler had spent a lifetime prying into the master's affairs. On the cold winter nights the butler entertained a crowd of servants, boastfully revealing the master's tales of illicit affairs with noble dames and with money.

"You fool, you're trickier than the devil." The butler shook his fist the day Ambrósio usurped his job, blackmailing his way from the Count's kitchen to the dining room. There, through many years, Ambrósio learned the power of eavesdropping to extort long-lasting influence and wealth.

The toll of bells pulled the procession up the hill towards the cemetery. Shuffled steps stirred the dust along the trail. Padre Lucas paced himself and the procession with the gospel's cadence.

"Blessed are the poor in spirit," prompted Padre Lucas.

"For theirs is the kingdom of heaven," responded the crowd.

Padre Lucas' suffering was visible in his blushing cheeks, a glow matched by the fruit of the wild raspberry bushes lining the trail.

> *"Blessed are they who mourn,*
> *for they will be comforted.*
> *Blessed are the meek,*
> *for they will inherit the land."*

The few peasants labouring amid the corn stalks stopped and stared. Their faces glistened with a mixture of dirt and sweat. At once beautiful and delicate, rough and painful, these corn stalks, irrigated by the sweat of their brows, flourished like bramble. Landless, they returned half of their crop to the Senhor who had generously permitted them to cultivate the land.

> *"Blessed are they who hunger and thirst for righteousness, for they will be satisfied. Blessed are they who are persecuted for theirs is the kingdom of heaven…"*

As the procession passed, the peasant women fell to their knees while the peasant men stood holding hats to their chests. They blessed themselves, in the name of the Father, the Son, and the Holy Spirit, tracing an imaginary cross from their foreheads to their chests. Even the pasturing cattle, black and white dots decorating the green valley tapestry, perpetually staring at the ground, lifted their heads and stared at the chorus of prayer, "Pray for us sinners, now and at the hour of our death. Amen."

The procession crossed the wooden bridge and youngsters cannonballed into the cool waters, spraying their mothers who were kneeling on the shore among steeples of clothes. Their plunges sent bubbles floating to the surface. Freshly washed sheets stretched over blackberry bushes soaking up the sun's dryness. A breeze lifted them slightly, a respectful nod of acknowledgement at the funeral's passage.

The graveyard within sight, the procession shuffled along the *levadas*, irrigation channels as deep as graves carrying life to the distant fields. Here children converged, racing boats fashioned from pine bark. The same place where infants of unwed servant mothers seemed unusually prone to accidental drownings.

Ambrósio had returned to his village of birth to take possession of the Count's summer mansion, a place for the declining aristocracy to pursue outdoor pleasures: hunting foxes, partridges and the increasingly elusive wolves. The mansion loomed tall over the villagers and the church.

Even though Ambrósio had found a wife to manage the domestic affairs, Ambrósio reserved the screening of servants to himself, a process he undertook with the utmost care. He believed the remedy against bitter surprises was prevention. "Every stone found in a well-sifted crop today, will save a tooth tomorrow," he was known to say.

In his male servants, he searched for those who dared not meet him in the eye, those eager to please, vacant of dreams and aspirations of their own. Aspirations were the seeds of ambition, which Senhor Ambrósio feared might topple him in the end. In the women, he searched for tender flesh barely in the threshold of womanhood. He had the caprice of selecting young poor women for whom the occasional use of their bodies was little price to pay in exchange for the meagre salary sustaining their families. He picked women that satisfied the good measure of his cupped hand.

Time and time again, Ambrósio had set out on foot with his faithful black umbrella in hand to provide escape from the scorching sun. "Only from up there," he reasoned, his umbrella pointing towards a solitary puff of cloud in the sky, "might uncontrollable surprises fall." Ambrósio enjoyed the protective shadow cast by his umbrella as he progressed up the hill searching for the stone shack of his childhood. The shack was hidden somewhere in the woods, where he had competed with foxes and other forest animals for shelter and cover from the Senhores' guns.

When he found the shack, moss brightened collapsed stone mounds where once crooked walls had risen. He surveyed the roof scattered about by fierce winter winds. He stumbled upon the family gravesite, a shallow pit filled with stones from the disintegrated house. A charitable soul, a hunter, another squatter perhaps, had found a moment to scratch a grave and to weave a cross of twigs, saving Ambrósio's family from clouds of flies. He used his naked hands to remove their remains and placed them in a burlap sack.

In the village graveyard he ordered construction of a mausoleum, chiselled from the purest marble. There he rested their ossified bodies in luxurious comfort. Every month he paid for a Mass in their tribute and ordered roses deposited at the foot of the tomb, honouring his mother. A woman of unrelenting optimism, a fervent believer in saintly miracles, struggling every morning to watch the sun rise, believing that every day was a new day, delivering fresh hope. A woman of unshakeable faith, convinced that the Heavens would hear her supplications and bring mercy. But the days unfolded indifferently, until their wilted bodies collapsed on a winter morning, clasped together so tightly that Ambrósio found them buried as one.

The procession gathered around the Mateus' grave site and before the Liturgy of Final Farewell, Padre Lucas asked those present to ponder on how Senhor Ambrósio had inspired them through his life on earth to deepen their faith in each other. A moment of silence ensued. Padre Lucas prayed.

"Let us pray to the Lord also for ourselves. May we who mourn be reunited one day with our brother; together may we meet Christ Jesus when He who is our life appears in glory."

The casket was lowered. In silence, the peasants watched Mário throw a rose into the dark pit where the petals would wilt and drop but the thorns would remain intact. The peasants turned as one and shuffled back to the sweaty fields. Mário, assisted by the

Senhores, returned to the Mateus mansion. Padre Lucas stood alone by the mouth of the grave.

He tossed a handful of soil onto the casket, raised his hand, blessing Senhor Ambrósio's eternal home. Then Padre Lucas blessed himself, cleared his throat, and watched as the spittle landed in the dark pit.

GARDEN OF DREAMS

Felismina Alves caught sight of the silhouettes skimming the lip
of the slope and, had word not spread warning of their inten-
tion to pay her a visit that Sunday, she might have mistaken
them for wild animals. But no. She was prepared. She would not
shut her door in anyone's face, not even theirs.

In the enveloping dusk Felismina sliced the last carrot. Onion
and garlic already sizzled in the soup pot. The sound competed with
the cicadas chirping in the meadow outside her kitchen window.
Felismina had spread wide the windows of her household. She invited the wind's faint whisper inside the chalk walls, and the wind swept
out trapped embers of hot air. Perhaps to seek refuge in the shelter of
the walls or perhaps attracted by the smell of sweet vermicelli cooling
on the table, flies sailed on the breeze and invaded the house. Felismina
sliced strings of kale and dropped them into the pot with the turnip. A
mixture of green and orange colours, of bitter and sweet flavours, sim-
mered, enriching her soup. Next Felismina sliced the potatoes while
her eye followed the outline of a wolf traversing the ravine. Protected
by shadows, the wolf warily approached the stream to quench its
thirst. The wolf flinched at the smell of the silhouettes that tinged the
air and Felismina watched as it fled into the shadows.

GARDEN OF DREAMS

The knock on the door.

"Hello. Are you Felismina Alves?"

"Yes, come in. What brings you to my door?" Felismina offered the guest and the accompanying child a stool. She seated herself on a log.

"The word of the Lord Almighty."

Felismina observed her out of breath guest. Her once immaculate linen dress was tucked between her knees, revealing a scraped shin. Traces of leaves and grass nested in her poorly dyed hair. Streaks of dirt ran lengthwise at the hips where she had wiped her hands. Felismina's guest was not a heavenly sight. On the contrary, her distressed soul appeared to need immediate salvation. Her daughter, carrying the same up-turned nose, huddled close to fit under the wing of her mother's arm. The poor creature was as frightened as a newborn duckling.

"Sorry to arrive at this late hour. We lost the threadlike trail. I never thought I would find someone dwelling so far from everyone else."

"What matters is your safe arrival," Felismina said, wiping her hands on her black apron. In the same breath she added, "Will you have soup?"

"Yes please, it smells delicious!" The woman's nose wriggled to catch the rising scent of olive oil.

"And for everyone finishing a bowl of soup there will be sweet vermicelli after." Felismina winked at the child.

The child anchored her gaze on the comfort of the glowing coals.

"Sweet vermicelli! That's very kind. "The woman squinted around the room struggling to discern her whereabouts. "You don't seem to mind the dark."

"Been accustomed to it all my life. Darkness isn't so black once our eyes warm up to it." Felismina scooped out a ladle overflowing with soup.

"Wouldn't cost much to bring electricity up here. A world

would open up for you. Refrigerator, television, even a washing machine to spare your chilblained hands."

Felismina enjoyed the dimness. It gave her peace of mind to realise the clouding of her ageing eyes brought no tragedy to her daily life. She moved confidently around the shadowed kitchen. What did she need from the glare of lights? Her fingers manoeuvred the sharp knives, fondling the memory of a thousand soups. Her bare feet read the wooden floor, avoided the water vessel, and anticipated a nail sticking its snobbish head above the others.

"Electricity?" Felismina said at last, dipping a spoon in the bowl and blowing the steam. "You sound like my oldest visiting at Easter full of modern advice. No, don't need any of those electrical vices. They only bring worries, more work. God gave us the night for a reason. So we can leave the land alone and be with each other."

In the night, dew collecting on the small of her back, Felismina had conceived; in the shade of her womb she had carried her children. In the daylight she lost them to the city; like her lush and bountiful garden where seeds germinated in the moist, black depth before reaching for the sun. The roots remained beneath the touch of light so they could send the green, season after season. Sacrifice to the mouth of the famished world.

"But a radio to listen to the affairs of the world and a telephone for emergencies aren't frivolous. They are basic necessities."

"Bread and water are basic necessities, dear. Look at Arturito, my youngest, toiling into the night under those light bulbs, burning the life out of his eyes. Hardly married and showing as many blanched hairs as my husband had when he passed away. It's no good. But I'm talking too much. Tell me what brings you here."

The woman straightened her back and tilted her chin upwards as if ceremoniously delivering a speech.

"Yes, yes of course. Our congregation visits people to bring them the truth about God. Like Jesus Himself said, I am the way, the truth and the light. Let there be light. I'm a humble servant of

23

God, that's all. Here's a gift." From her purse she removed a beeswax candle wrapped in religious pamphlets. The honey-sweet fragrance permeated the air.

"That's lovely. I'm a humble servant myself, tending this little corner of God's garden."

The coals, turned cinder, ceased to spread a glow of comfort and abandoned Felismina's guests to the blackness. That was just as well with Felismina. She found reassurance in darkness. In summer she sat on the wild grass, paying court to the constellations. In her imagination she travelled far, entering distant worlds, catching revealing glimpses into the mysteries of the night. She always returned from the enigmatic skies empty handed, lacking the simplest confirmation to her questions. But she arrived fresh, unlike the fatigued, weary traveller in her kitchen weighed down with books and pamphlets and arriving with simple answers, preaching universal truths.

"As good Christians it's our obligation to rescue every soul from hell by spreading the Word."

Felismina brought a spoonful of soup to her mouth and slurped with gusto before speaking.

"I see, you go from kitchen to kitchen telling people their potatoes must be cubed rather than sliced because they are better for you that way!" Felismina smiled.

A breeze bumped the window. An owl hooted. The child's teeth chattered.

"Darkness frightens my daughter. Maybe we should light this?" The woman still held the candle in her hand.

"If it will make you feel better, dear." Felismina snapped her thick callused fingers in a loud crack, producing a spark to light the wick.

The child's eyes widened. She huddled closer to her mother who attempted to comfort her with a nervous grin.

As the flicker of light inundated the room, the sleepy flies sharpened their wings, fooled by the belief of a new day rising.

They circled the women's heads in short tentative flights, some promptly returning to the rafters. Others, attracted by the wavering flame, the single source of light, dove towards the flare.

A sizzling crackle. In silence the women contemplated the fly, legs twitching in the hot wax.

Felismina recalled an image of her father stumbling around the house on his obstinate quest for enlightenment, for heaven. In the mid-day haze, his search had led him to stare intently at the sunlight. The brighter the sun, the heavier the shadow, Felismina concluded and lived her life by that measure.

The child cringed at the sizzling of the fly's flesh in the flame. She clung to her mother, clutched her hand. Through the window streamed the cadenza of cicadas.

Felismina stood up and gathered the empty soup bowls. She cut a large square of sweet vermicelli and served her guests.

"Come outside girl," Felismina said, extending an inviting hand, "I'll show you my garden of stars."

The child looked at her mother for permission. Her mother nodded in assent. The three, dessert plates in hand, walked outside. Felismina knelt while the two sat on upright logs savouring their sweet vermicelli, watching Felismina build a tiny pyre of dry pine needles. A firefly danced around Felismina, departing as soon as the first flame licked the air.

Flame after flame, the fire spread and devoured the logs. The graceful faces of sunflowers gleamed against the sky. Felismina, sitting cross-legged on the grass, pinched a leaf from a sage cluster and rubbed it between her palms, drawing in a long breath of the sweet fragrance. She threw the leaf into the crackling flames and sang about riding the skies on the tail of a comet. The cicadas joined in. The hoot of the owl marked tempo and fireflies circled them in a dance.

"See there dear, that's the Little Dipper, looking just like the ladle we used to scoop the soup." Felismina retrieved a twig from the fire and traced the Dipper's profile in the air with the incandescent tip.

The child smiled.

"Can you spot that shiny star by the handle's tail?"

The child nodded.

"That's Polaris, a cheerful one in the night. It'll guide any lost soul to safety."

"How did the stars get there?"

Felismina sat by the fire smiling, warming her callused hands above the flames. Then she poked the fire and a spray of sparkles ascended.

The child's eyes widened, shone brighter with understanding.

"New stars are born everyday, everywhere. They'll rise and rise through cosmic dust until they find a patch of sky they like. And up there, far in the heavens, they'll nestle among the galaxies waiting for people, animals and flowers to join them one day."

On Felismina's meadow, the night stars lent gentle contours to the landscape before daylight blanched the world once again. The night, where tree limb and owl merged, was impossible to define. The night, where stones moulded themselves into the profiles of wild animals and sat quietly, ready to jump. The night, ambiguous, giving birth to dreams, to the impossible. To life.

"Mother, is heaven where I'll go after I die?" The child asked pointing at the night sky.

"Yes, you'll go somewhere above the clouds."

"Is that true Ti Felismina?"

"Yes dear, when you die you go wherever you believe you go."

"Then I'll soar like a star!" The child exclaimed with conviction, jumping in the air, spreading her arms with a resolved celestial gaze.

"You'll soar then."

"And where will you go?"

"Ahhh dear, I'll stay. I'll burrow underground and slowly grow up to be a sunflower, waiting for the bees to tickle my petals."

"Where will you go, mother?"

The woman sighed, shifted on the unsteady log.

"I'll go wherever God tells me to go."

The women, heads heavenwards, stared at the speckled sky. A light breeze fanned the flames. The mother shifted her log around the fire to escape the smoke but it followed her wherever she moved. Not far away a wolf howled at the crescent moon. A log hissed loudly. A hurried light slashed the sky.

"What was that?" the child asked, startled.

"A shooting star. Sometimes stars tire of being stars and return to earth to become children, fireflies, owls." As Felismina spoke, her hand swept the air and closed. She held her sealed hand in her lap like a secret. "Guess what I have in my hand?"

"I know, I know," the child jumped up from her log and clapped. She turned to her mother. "Look, she caught the falling star in her hand!"

The mother threw a dismissive laugh.

The child crouched next to Felismina on the grass, her radiant face above Felismina's curled fingers.

Felismina released her fingers one by one to reveal the motionless star blinking in her palm. She raised her hand and tossed the star in the air. The star did not soar. Instead, it orbited around them like a moon describing a beautiful circle dance. The child rested her head on the tip of her pressed hands and followed the dance in awe. Soon the women were surrounded by constellations of stars.

The woman stood up.

"We must go now. This is enough."

"But I like it here. It's too far to go home now."

The mother stared into the blinding darkness, then at the fire. She slowly lowered herself onto her seat, fanning the smoke in her face with a religious pamphlet.

A Millstone,
Always a Millstone

The blessed water trickled upon the infant's sleep, pronouncing him Maria das Dores.* His cry of betrayal echoed in the serene sanctuary, pleading upwards to the gothic columns, where it ricocheted from the stone ears of the Saints, deaf from centuries of parishioners' petitions.

Padre Lucas proceeded with the baptismal ceremony, his austere voice disregarding Maria das Dores' supplications.

"I shall remove the heart of stone from your body
and give you a heart of flesh.
I shall place my spirit in you,
and make you keep my laws
and sincerely respect my observances."

Maria das Dores, for consolation, moulded his tiny body closer in his mother's arms, just as the clay vases on the altar had moulded themselves in the moistened hands of their creators.

Engulfed in black, Eufémia, the infant's mother, was a pic-

* Mary of the Suffering

29

ture of burnt devastated soil delivering from her bosom the delicate white rose of his being. She prayed silently.

> *"Lord, you have blessed me with this precious life.*
> *May Maria das Dores grow in the discovery of truth.*
> *May her hands be used to transform this world.*
> *May her eyes never be closed to those in need."*

Eufémia's silent lips raced in a string of prayers that sought forgiveness. The insanity of pain had condemned her to intervene in matters traditionally reserved to Divinities. A humble servant of God, she prayed to attenuate the immeasurable misfortunes of the world, and certain that God would approve of her decision to raise her son under the habits of a girl.

With the death of her husband, Eufémia had vowed to protect Maria das Dores, her sweet bundle of innocence, from the predatory mandibles of the world. Had her gentle giant man been present, she was certain he would have approved of her desperate, yet immaculately intentioned efforts to intervene in Divine matters.

Acácio had been a sacrificial lamb. His only sin hung between his legs, enabling him the pleasure that had fathered his child, and in the end, also sentenced him to death.

Conscription had arrived, stomping through the courtyard, kicking the kitchen door open, as it had for Acácio's forefathers who had been snatched in the night and sent to the Crusades to slaughter and perish in distant lands not their own. And again, in Acácio's time, flesh was being herded into the jaws of Europe to bleed a war in a strange land, a strange language. He resisted destiny, concealed in the salt chest with the quartered pork, while the house was searched. The following day he sold trowel, square and plumb line—the tools of his trade. He borrowed money, desperate to trick death pending in the battlefield. He bribed his escape, smuggled inside an oak chest destined for Brazil. Brazil, land of dreams and riches. He dreamed of returning alive and wealthy. From the departing Pandora's box his hand had blown Eufémia a hopeful kiss. A lone candle burned next to the font, piercing the darkness of the church. Maria das Dores persevered in his loud protest. The water's icy fingers lingered on his forehead, the scattered droplets seared his tender skin. Padre Lucas hastened through the christening. "May the Lord Jesus touch your ears to receive His word, and your mouth to proclaim His faith, to the praise and glory of God." Padre Lucas' thumb touched the ears and mouth of Maria das Dores. He ended by signalling the cross on the infant's forehead.

Eufémia scurried home, her legs slicing the fog that blanketed the village. At home, by the hearth, sloping forward on her stool and holding Maria das Dores under one arm, she built a fire to combat the shivers that refused to leave her life. Shivers, reminiscent of the haunted night, weeks earlier, when she had received word of Acácio's death. Snuggled to the flames, smoke stinging her eyes, her hands had rested on the hill of her stretched womb.

"The will of God," the messenger from her estranged and unwilling father, had suggested.

"What kind of a God locks one of his souls in a chest, in the hold of a cargo ship, burying his dreams alive," she yelled.

Meaningless words to ease her tears. Tears, a torrent that sent pots whirling in the air and glass spraying from the walls, the way rivers smash water against rock. The tempest broke her dammed waters and grief drowned under the flood of birthing pain.

Sunday. As distant church bells announced the end of Mass, Eufémia's last visitor hurried back home. In her arms, Maria das Dores cried. Eufémia stepped into the cold river behind her shack to scrub away the sweat that impregnated her skin. Her breasts ached from many unshaven faces. Eufémia unbuttoned her

31

blouse and brought Maria das Dores to her nipple. The infant quieted. Eufémia splashed water between her thighs and sang the *Fado* in a mournful voice, a melancholic wail rising from the depths of her aches.

> *"River of crystal waters*
> *on your way to the sea*
> *the torments that I bear*
> *confide not to thee."*

Her tears floated down, a day's journey to the Atlantic, where she believed the grief of the world was preserved in a gigantic vat of brine. The pure and crystallised pain of the less fortunate, floating away, destined to return one day as spice for privileged and refined palates.

On Monday, the river saw the village wives converge, folded at their knees, slapping their husband's underpants against stone slabs, their red hands numb from the cold water. The wives' fists wrung their husband's undershirts at the collars until they bled strange scents of pleasure. The silent stained water, without a ripple of discontent, purged the clothes and carried the dirt far from everyone's sight.

The Sunday Eufémia fulfilled the last of Acácio's unpaid debts, she walked to the waters, raw chin high and earthly duties honoured. At the water's edge she kneeled and examined her reflection. She agonised over the premature wrinkles, the white around her temples, the darkness around the eyes, the ghost she had become. Eufémia waded into the silky water and with each step her skirt rose and floated on the surface like a weeping black orchid huddling her torso and slowly closing its petals, swallowing her body. Eufémia's last tear merged with the current, and her grieving body finally withered from innumerable nights of lonely cries, beginning a pilgrimage that would end in the Atlantic brine, next to her beloved Acácio.

Upstream, Maria das Dores waited inside the watermill. He heard the gargling of water outside and the cooing of pigeons nesting on the rafters. Impatiently, he waited for his mother. A plate of salted lupini sat on a wrinkled, scribbled piece of paper Eufémia had slid underneath. Impeded by a knot in Maria das Dores' throat, the lupini were thrown mindlessly, one by one, under the crushing millstone. Maria das Dores despised Sundays. The men and the tobacco that filled his home.

Ambrósio, the wealthiest man in Vale D'Água Amargurada, crumpled the paper note in his hand and tossed it into the river. He took pity on the child of his relegated daughter, Eufémia. Eufémia had been the last of his hopes for a convenient union to an ageing landlord, before she fled his home to marry a poor stone mason and seek refuge amid the passion of bare walls. A man of strong beliefs and unmoveable will, Ambrósio dutifully welcomed the orphan under his protective wing. He stood above the girl, crouched by the river's edge, huddling her legs against her chest, tossing twigs into the water and following their journey with her withered gaze until they disappeared from view. "Come to your new home. You need a long hot scrub in a lavender bath." Ambrósio extended his hand and led the child up the trail through the grapevine terraces.

A shriek from a young female servant followed by her distressed call for aid, brought Ambrósio to the courtyard. There, held high beneath a apple tree, Maria das Dores hovered above the wooden tub. Her dangling legs were spread wide, the way Ambrósio might have found a vendor holding rabbits for inspection in the market. Ambrósio sauntered over to the child and tweaked his stump of flesh as if to confirm its existence. Maria das Dores screamed and shrivelled. Ambrósio rubbed his nose.

"Bury the past, all but an ugly dream. From today on you will answer to the name of Mário. Is that understood?"

The following day Maria das Dores' grandfather summoned a barber who shaved off his long braids leaving his head exposed to the merciless winter. It bared memories of bitter cold mornings, when the night remained trapped inside his mother's shack and frozen air like floating ice scraped his skin. Mornings he had watched the futile efforts of the infant fire, its tiny serrated teeth of flames, sawing, sawing at the frozen air. Mornings his mother had sat on a stool by the fire, as close to flames as she could sit for comfort, waiting until the iron kettle boiled and steaming barley thawed their flesh. Mornings his mother French braided his hair, pulling and twisting at three strands while singing.

> "Oh, River of crystal waters
> on your way to the sea
> the torments that I bear
> confide not to thee."

After Maria das Dores' braids vanished, his grandfather summoned the best tailor in the village to fit him with a suit that corralled his body, and a tie that lassoed his neck, strangling his voice.

Maria das Dores was forced to gather his dresses in a pile, next to a mound of weeds from the garden. Before the glare of his menacing grandfather, Mário's trembling hands ignited the match that turned the past into smoke.

Tears in his eyes, staring at the crackling flames, Mário realised that the days of hopscotch in the company of girlfriends, leaping from square to square with grace and deftness, were over. He already missed the fresh air, twirling inside his red pleated skirt, kissing his thighs with featherlike lips. He missed the fingers of sunshine, caressing his knees, leaving a residual tingle on his skin. He had been sentenced to the ferocity of boy's games, to bruised skin and bloodied skull. His legs trembled and his stomach heaved over the fire.

Later that day, his grandfather obliged him to collect chicken excrement. A fastidious task around the yard until a jar was filled. His grandfather stood erect against the orange tree and ordered Mário to spread the excrement in a thick layer over his chest, "Be generous," his grandfather instructed, "better safe than sorry. After all, it is fertilising your manhood." Then over the cheeks and chin because it was the best fertiliser a man would find, as his grandfather proved by showing the bush on his chest, and crediting it to the intervention of his own father at an age comparable to Mário's.

Mário detested his grandfather's outhouse. He escaped the vigilant eyes of his grandfather and by retreating into the corner of the garden, behind the green beans climbing up the tall trestles, where he squatted the way his mother had taught him. He wrestled his pants, locking him at the ankles, upsetting his balance and invariably splattered his legs. He ignored the sprayed pants. He would rather linger there, squatting, protected by the curtain of bean foliage. His eyes followed a world unravelling at the pace of a snail; a potato beetle trotting up a blade of grass, soon to be airborne. Then, a trail of ants, a frantic to and fro, a wavering black thread mending the earth's seams, preventing it from tearing. He preferred squatting next to the apple tree, not losing sight of life among the grasses.

There, squatting behind the bean trestles, he overheard a gathering of his grandfather's field hands discussing the tragedy of his Father's death. Acácio and countless other fugitives, vulnerable in the illegality of their escape, had become slaves labouring in the hell of a ship's coal furnace. As the silhouette of the Brazilian landscape had spun into view, the stars had shut their eyes to the pushed bodies struggling to stay afloat in the shark infested waters.

"Can always count on finding someone to profit from the dreams and fears of the poor." There was a clamour of agreement. Someone else continued, "And the rich, God lets them, pay their way out of wars."

Mário's legs trembled like fragile corn shoots in a field. He collapsed backwards. Poverty was a curse; a downfall he must avoid at any cost.

On the dining room table, an olive oil lantern stood between Mário and his grandfather. Mário answered his hunger with corn bread, avoiding the bowl of pumpkin soup facing him.

Ambrósio, on alert for opportunities to improve Mário's character, noted the boy's aversion to pumpkin soup. He ordered the servants to provide Mário with nothing but three daily bowls of soup. A temporary measure that ended when Mário pronounced, from his own free will, thankful appreciation for pureed pumpkin. "Hunger is the best spice," his grandfather proclaimed. He reasoned a man was created to overcome the unpleasantries of life, wrestling challenges the way one wrestled a bull. Taking it by the horns and forcing it to kneel in submission. "The day of victory arrives when the mind overcomes the body and reason overcomes the emotions." His grandfather's voice thundered and his fist hammered the table, overturning his empty wine mug.

36

Ambrósio stood and paced the perimeter of the table, arms locked behind his back. He stopped behind Mário. Then he stooped over him. Mário held his breath. He felt the hot wind blowing out of his grandfather's nostrils, burning the nape of his neck. "A man in your position and of your wealth, should expect to face a life of unpleasantness. A steady hand of iron, free from sentimentality, is mandatory to expand our accumulated riches. It is a man's job." Ambrósio's expectant hand landed on Mário's shoulder.

Returning from the open market, eating the distance with his youthful steps, Mário crossed paths with one of the poor villagers, a bastard of bastards, rescued from starvation by a woman of strict religious beliefs. Mário recognised the vacant eyes of an orphan. He was enamoured by her sadness and apologetic smile, the crepuscular eyes that requested so little from life. Mário turned. He walked toward the market again, following the tapping of her clogs on stone. In the market she stopped at the dried fish stall to buy tails of salted cod. Mário stepped into the neighbouring fish stall and ordered a grilled sardine with a piece of corn bread. He leaned on a pole, watched as she entered the cloth merchant's stall. She slid her fingers over the silks, pausing at the reds. She held a luscious red strip against her body, but she set it back and turned to the linen. She weighed an arm's full of linen. In his daydreaming, Mário embraced her, rocked her in his arms, fantasising the love and protection he would give her.

At his gate, Ambrósio waited for his grandson's return from the market. He chewed a mouthful of tobacco and spit the mush across the road. In his absorption, he did not tip his hat in greeting as neighbours passed by. Word of Mário's adolescent affections had reached Ambrósio's ears swifter than the warning of a frosty north wind.

Mário sighted his grandfather at the gate and he arrived staring at his now dull leather shoes.

"I see you've taken to wearing smart shoes. Let's hope you continue to deserve the shoes you wear."

Mário remained silent.

"She has an eye on your inheritance. You ought to be investing your interest in the Neves' daughters, well endowed women." Mário's grandfather aimed his attention less at their fleshy chests than at their dowry chests, which promised generous expanses of land as well as rivers of milk and honey.

Mário, under threats of being disowned, was strictly forbidden to approach her.

Torn between the longing in his heart and the comfort of his flesh, Mário buried his dreams of eloping with Maria da Saudade.* The threat of his destitute past, the plain barley, the iced breath, and the disturbing story of his father's destiny echoing in his ears, made him cling to the comfort and privileges under his grandfather's roof.

Nevertheless, Mário and Maria da Saudade's relationship flourished in the pale glow of the moon, beneath the umbrella of grapevines or the roof of corn stalks, growing stronger in the whispers of furtive encounters. In his impatience, he kneeled by the side of his bed and prayed to Our Lady of Fátima, her faded yellowed smile hanging above his bed. He prayed for a merciful end to his grandfather's heart.

"Remember, O most gracious Virgin Mary, never was it known that anyone who fled to your protection, implored your help, or sought your intercession, was left unaided."

Patient as the ox, quiet as the owl, Mário obediently brought to his grandfather his bedtime Lemon Balm tea. He watched as his health deteriorated, until finally, Ambrósio's ageing bones fell prisoner to the confines of a bed, leaving Mário tenuously chained to his wilful breathing. Mário continued to pray.

With his path unencumbered, Mário applied himself to preparing his long awaited union with Maria da Saudade. He planned the merriest wedding in the valley. He fattened up pigs, chickens and cows. A tun of his best wine was placed aside. He had a suit tailored to accommodate his increasing plumpness, with a tie to match. All was proceeding favourably until Padre Lucas, flipping through his church records, recalled baptising Mário a quarter of a century back. He declared in the name of moral righteousness and Divine decency, that he could not pronounce Maria das Dores and Maria da Saudade, wife and... wife.

"I have called you by your name, you are mine," Padre Lucas quoted Isaiah and reminded Mário that in the Last Judgement God would call everyone by name. To Padre Lucas, it was evident Mário continued to be Maria das Dores in the eyes of God.

"This whole affair is a blasphemy." Padre Lucas fumed. This mingling of Marys challenged well-established rules of procreation. His ecclesiastic training had not prepared him for such a calamity.

Despair settled upon the couple as they realised their tribulations had just begun. It was no longer the will of one stubborn man, Mário's grandfather. It was the chasm of centuries of tradition and religious mores, petrified into customs, that barred them from uniting their lives.

Mário pursued his last recourse, an appeal to the ultimate divine authority on earth. His plea was accompanied by a generous donation to facilitate the expression of God's will, and with a lick of his tongue his reverent petition was sealed. Their destiny

* Mary of the Longing

39

deposited into the hands of the Pope.

After Mass, on Sundays, awaiting the Pope's verdict, Mário and Maria da Saudade huddled by the watermill. They stared at the heaviness of the millstone carving its customary course, following a deep rut, around and around in smooth circles. They tossed salted lupini onto the millstone and watched the tender flesh heartlessly crushed.

The Scent of a Lie

We never carried ill intentions towards Camila Penca. We simply prayed for our village's old peace to be restored and, thank God, He answered our prayers.

Camila was born into a well-bred family in our respectable village nestled on the tusk-sharp escarpment of Hell's Mouth Bay. A village still standing with pride and resilience after centuries of Atlantic rage. Camila spent childhood in her own world. She climbed up and down the escarpment, collecting gull feathers, splashing in the tide pools, plucking at the sea urchins, 'she loves me, she loves me not,' then, with the first tides of puberty, 'he loves me, he loves me not.'

Some say that all along Camila displayed an inclination to stir up havoc. Surely there were instances of wickedness, as she had spied on people in their outhouses or stood on other girls' chests to help them muscle up breasts. But who has never been possessed by wicked moments?

Mostly, we blamed the late Ti Bernardino Mudo for leaving the mouth of his old well broad to the sky. Trapped at the bottom, the smells of the rotting wooden foundation, the sweet moss and the salty ocean mist tingling her nose, Camila crouched in a puddle, peering at a sky that resembled an eye. Not even the waves' consoling murmur found her ears. Gulls and rats were her only company. Gulls hopping from beam to beam above her head and sprinkling earth crumbs on her hair, rats scurrying over her body for a fish bone.

Lord, forgive us for such evil thoughts, but one would almost have wished Camila had never survived that cursed hole. We searched the land. We launched fishing nets and combed the bay, in the hope her body lay entangled in the sargasso. We peeked into the cleavages of rock for her trapped body. All without luck. Her mother, waiting on the beach with the moon and the stars, wailed the child's body ashore, as months before she had waited for the breakers to return her husband. It was she who spotted the green balloon tied to the gull, swooping and diving above the cliffs, against the rising sun. Camila had carried a green balloon in her pocket since she was knee high, "will lift me one day into the sky like Icarus," she would sing.

The gull led us to Camila and we fished her out of the damp well. Everyone wanted to touch and kiss the girl. Mayor Ressaca, full of pomp and reeking of cologne, eeled through the pandemonium and covered her in kisses. His thunderous voice promised he would name a village lane after Camila, a lane parallel to her father's as soon as the new roads were paved in his next mandate. Padre Baptista blessed Camila, assuring her he had known all along she was in the safe hands of God. Dona Branca told her she had prayed the rosary nightly and Camila would not have to worry about school work again. Camila fidgeted and sneezed. She told us to stop. She could smell our fishy lies. We laughed. A fall from such height was known to stir funny things in one's mind. Her wide terrified eyes focused above our heads and her steady sneezing went unnoticed in the midst of the tumult over her rescue.

After years of surrendering villagers to the sea and losing hope in miracles, we gathered for Mass, thanking the Trinity and the Virgin Mary for protecting a Christian soul and returning a village child safely to our lap. Padre Baptista's homily reeled-in the virtues of Christian faith. He assured the congregation that Camila's successful rescue was God's reward to the few spirits who attended his nightly rosaries and resisted the Devil's traps in Ti Inácio's tavern maids. The Devil tempted the flesh into dark holes. Camila began to sneeze relentlessly, crying "Lie well." The perplexed Padre Baptista on the pulpit blushed, and Sister Maria, in the choir, stared at her habit.

We stopped Mass and wrapped Camila in a winter blanket assuming the dampness of the well had brought on her infernal sneezing.

Before re-assembling for Mass we demanded that Camila confess her sins. We obliged her to purge any unattended sin that might have caused our Lord to inflict her with such penance. We huddled around the confessional. We heard her confide to Padre Baptista that she could smell a lie. Some lies were masked under perfumes, others hid under cow manure. Dressed in perfume or cow manure, every lie carried the subtlest yet unmistakable stench of rotting fish, which triggered a gull-like cry from deep inside Camila's being. When she remembered the Act of Contrition we sighed, relieved.

Returning to the Mass, we sniffed the air. There was no stench of rotting fish. Only the sweet beeswax candles dripping and the rose scent of incense from the altar. We could not even blame Rosária Cardo, the fishmonger. Rosária Cardo who would rush into the pews late, wiping her hands on her hips, glistening sardine scales clinging to her skirt. But Rosária Cardo was away on her Friday run into neighbouring villages, at that moment she was likely balancing her wicker basket along a winding goat trail.

Ti Raul said perhaps it was his fault. After changing into his Sunday clothes for the Mass, he had been unable to stop himself

43

from checking the crab traps on his way to church. The smells might have clung to his best suit.

Padre Baptista exercised his God-given authority and led Camila by the wrist to the pulpit. Under the Virgin Mary's statue he tested Camila's claims. He began by telling her that Adamastor, the sea-monster, was denned in our bay, as was the commonly held belief. Camila's nose twitched upwards, faster and faster, until three sneezes bellowed out, accompanied with the cry "Lie well," announcing to us a lie had dropped in the village, wet as a splash of guano. Padre Baptista smiled approvingly. He also told her that one of the Virgin's three secrets at Fátima was the world's imminent end. Camila's sneezing rung through the church, echoing like three strikes of the church bell. Padre Baptista muttered his assent and blessed himself. He was convinced. At that moment we thought Camila was heaven's messenger, a blessing.

Padre Baptista finished Mass with the choir ceaselessly singing in the background. He sacrificed his words of wisdom, but he knew it was best to fill the air with a storm of words. That way he could always point his finger at the choir any time Camila's sneezing might threaten to ripple biblical waters. Padre Baptista's inspired solution prompted our Hail Mary of thanks. Later, Mayor Ressaca, encouraged by Padre Baptista's success, never again discussed the village's budget without Dona Branca reading the newspaper aloud in the background.

As Camila slowly recovered from her ordeal in the well, she confided to us she could smell lies gathering above our heads the way we could see a summer storm gathering over the top of the Serra do Senhor Frutuoso.

Day or night, we had never a moment of peace. It was as if a thick fog had moved in from the sea and settled over the village. The trumpeting of Camila's nose echoed against the cliffs, down the cobblestone streets and entered a home without knocking. Even the whispers of husbands and wives in the matrimonial bed were not immune to Camila's nose. Ti Justa and Ti António, after fifty years happily married, cut relations as Ti Justa threw Ti António's pillow into the corral with the goats. In bed he had been whispering honeyed words, "My sweet Justa, my life's true and only love," just as a sneeze sounded, freezing their beads of amorous sweat. Ti António's mouth, caught in the open, left Ti Justa forever cursed with doubt. Husband or wife could never agree if the lie, like a crow of bad luck, perched in another bedroom or their own. Couples would argue into the black over who was lying and about what.

We started to walk around the village like ghosts, our eyes swollen, irritated at the least uphill difficulty. The Mudos and the Silvas, families firmly entwined from century-old blood alliances, refused to speak to one another and forbade their children from playing together. All because Marcelino Mudo, standing in line at the bakery, demanded aloud from Carolina Silva the yearly kiss she had promised him during their teenage dating years. Carolina Silva gathered her twin toddlers on each hip and stomped out yelling to Marcelino Mudo once and for good keep his gossipy tongue to himself or go kiss the sea urchins instead.

We would not chance speaking alone. To avoid catching a tongue out of its element, conversations unrolled with everyone rallying at once. We didn't lend an ear to one another. The village affairs began to crumble. A tongue caught flapping during one of Camila's sneezing attacks was instantly sentenced to the fate of a sole on land—hung up to dry under a cloud of doubt. For Camila warned us, the seven deadly sins were like a deep well, and lying was the lid that prevented their expiation. Layers and layers of sins rotted in the dark of the deep and a sin was never born alone. There were always strings and bait.

Having a mere child flog us like sinners was not a fish-bone the village was prepared to swallow. That was between God and

45

oneself. Sins were a private business and no one walked through life without netting a full catch. But when many people commit a sin, together, then we are talking evil and that is something else.

Ti Raul, mending the nets on the beach, suggested it wasn't poor Camila's fault. She was a celestial angel. A true guardian angel, keeping us on course, saving us from drowning in eternal hell. He insisted that if we only committed to tell the truth to each other we would find joy and peace. Marcelino Mudo, leaning on the prow of his boat, always ready to stir sand in the air with his sting-ray tongue, told Ti Raul his mussel-brain notions were crazy. Everyone needed cover from the punishing world. Ti Raul, pointing at the sea, held that we went fishing in the open, where there was nowhere to hide, facing wind, fog and rain, but we survived. Marcelino Mudo snorted he was forgetting the drowned. Ti Raul kissed the gold cross dangling from his chest and stared at the fog-shrouded sky before declaring it was also our ignorance that caused us to drown. No one in the village had bothered to learn to swim. Ti António, until then silent, lifted his stocking cap to scratch his bald head and reminded Ti Raul that in fairness most of us didn't know we were not telling the truth because we had been whispering through nets for so long. The small-fry lies, like the air we breathed, had always escaped harmlessly through the nets. Marcelino Mudo moored the conversation, suggesting God was punishing us for old wrinkly sins.

We were nearing despair and might have committed something ungodly had we not set about restoring the peace in the village. With Padre Baptista's blessing, candlelight vigils gathered around Ti Bernardino's well, and incessant prayers were said to cleanse the rotten spirits that infested the dark hole. We even winched Camila down on a rope while Padre Baptista blessed her and the well with holy waters of the ocean, but to no avail. Her sneezing would not surrender. She bellied out in protest that it was the village and not she who needed to hang over the bottom of the rotten well to have a good look at themselves in the dark puddles. She insisted we were slippery eels hiding in the murky bottom. We lit more candles and prayed more fervently. Camila's last words were that we could never drown our conscience. The ocean waters returned things promptly. Poor child. We were trying to help.

The next morning the village woke up to silence. The fog had miraculously lifted. The ocean slept without a ripple, reflecting the blue of heaven. Even Esmeraldina, the young widow who had sworn never to show her face to daylight, opened her blinds a crack, curious about the oceanlike murmur of the crowd gathered in the square. Ti António remarked that the morning smelled of air after a storm, sweet and serene. Ti Raul, who had nearly drowned in his youth, said the still waters reminded him of the ocean's bottom. During storms, fishermen say the sea floor remains calm, and that is the reason our drowned reach the shore with a peaceful smile, but with no eyes. The deep-sea creatures steal their eyes. Eyes distract one from seeing the truth, seeing their way back to land. The sea creatures hide the eyes in tight-lipped shells where they harden into gleaming pearls only fit to admire one's vanity. Staring at the glimmering waters, Marcelino Mudo said we had reached bottom on this affair with Camila. Everyone agreed.

Camila was nowhere to be seen. We searched without luck. Dropped fishing nets. Combed the bay from shoulder to shoulder. Night and day, Camila's mother kneeled on the beach wailing her spirit to heaven. She plucked at sea urchins, 'hates me, hates me not.' Four of the strongest women in the village anchored her down as she wrestled, possessed by an urge to run into the ocean one moment, up the escarpment the next.

The gulls feeding out at sea shattered the aquatic mirror. An army of children with sling shots drove their cries away from Hell's Mouth Bay. One girl said she spotted a green balloon floating out to sea but we were all there and the morning light reflecting in the waters is known to play devilish tricks on the mind.

We will never know the mystery of God's wishes or the destiny of Camila Penca. We enjoy the old peace back in the village and have nailed down for good the mouth of Ti Bernardino's well.

Sardines and Acorns

The fishmonger's cry pierced Afonso's bedroom wall and woke him from the dullness of his dreams.

"Fresh. It's ocean fresh! Come, come. Taste for yourselves. From sea to mouth, a leap of joy!"

Women's clogs, hammering the paving stones, raised him out of bed swifter than one of Eulália's buckets of water.

Afonso opened the interior glass door of the balcony. He invited inside the voices climbing up the wall on the back of the mid-day air. The voices slid through the oak shutters. He returned to bed.

"Hurry folks hurry. Lively sardines and horse-mackerel belly-dancing on your plates."

Afonso cringed, picturing the reality of two-day-old sardines, their glazed eyes, their flaccid flesh. The clear eyes and bright scarlet gills of the freshly caught were a distant mirage.

He heard Eulália's heavy steps entering the room.

"The fishmonger's here. Want anything?"

"Some flounder would be nice…"

Ahh. The nerve! Pamper your royal palate when you can afford it." She swiftly seized a clog and pitched it at his head. He ducked under the covers. The clog hit the crucifix hanging on the wall. Better than a bucket of water, Afonso mused while Eulália

49

continued. "Lucky me if I can bargain for the leftovers. The bone-riddled sardines the neighbour's cat scorns."

"Sardines then." A better choice, Afonso thought. Sardines had plenty of bone, taking twice as long to eat, tricking the stomach into the illusion of an interminable feast. Even half-rotten sardines were a treat for mountain villagers. He remembered Fridays, standing knee-high to his mother, watching her scale sardines. When she finished, the fish scales clung to her widow's dress; gleaming stars on the black sky leading his gaze to the Milky Way.

The enclave of Comba, nested on the crown of a terraced hill, was so remotely poised that not even the lost souls down in Vale D'Água Amargurada wandered into the place. A flimsy threadlike trail, better fit for the hooves of wild animals than bare feet, only brought one weekly visitor; Rosária Cardo at the end of her run.

The noon sun seared the blanket of salt covering the fish trays, releasing ocean scents. Through Afonso's open window the freed ocean air climbed into his room and stirred hopes of prosperous years ahead. He imagined the sound of waves, the golden sand. Some day he and Eulália, for the sake of their children and their health, would embark on a seashore pilgrimage. The day's journey to Hell's Mouth Bay would be launched under the full moon to assure an early morning arrival. They would join the villagers with money to spare who once a year emptied into the sea. A trickle of people descending the mountain. A thin procession heading to the weekend festivities of Saint Bartholomew of the Sea. On the last day of celebrations he would dip his newborn into the ocean as a precaution against general diseases. If need be, he would bathe the child at length to cleanse specific curses—stuttering or epilepsy. If the wind howled and the surf foamed, the waters would be particularly effective to save an infant from the fear of fear. The waters were also renowned for promoting intelligence and good disposition. He would embrace the plunge into the waves, fully clothed, to renew the ocean's blessing and protection. Through the years protection could wear thin, and renewal was never excessive. On the return journey he and Eulália would walk stooped, weighed down by bags of salt which would fill their meat chests and preserve the pork through the winter. He stopped his reverie realizing that his children were yet to be born and he had yet to bathe in ocean waters.

It had been weeks since he laboured on the top terrace fields where a clear day offered him a glimpse of the distant shore. From up there he could hear Rosária Cardo. Her songs climbed up the trail, long before her varicose veins. She sang to herself beneath three layers of trays balanced on a coiled rag. Eventually, he could see the swing of her hips stirring salt atop the fish load. The crystals fell in a sprinkle around her. Soon women and men would drop their hoes and rush down to meet her in the village square.

Below Afonso's balcony, the commotion increased as more women arrived from the fields. Their voices drowned the sound of the small stream that gargled through his back yard. The women haggled over fish prices and freshness. He imagined the men within earshot sitting on the steps of the granite cross that filled the heart of the square. The men, pretending to mind their own business, twisted black berets in their hands, impatient to hear news of the outside world from Rosária Cardo.

"What's new from the lower lands, fish monger?"

"Salazar has sent word to every man in the nation, be he lame, blind or dumb, to join him in silencing the rebellions in the colonies." The worried clamour of the crowd rose above the dust. Rosária continued. "Through every village I've walked, no man has refused to answer Salazar's call."

"Even the men from Hell's Mouth Bay?" someone asked, prompting wide spread laughter. Bay men were renowned for never missing an invitation to fight.

"We will send our men to defend us," agreed a woman and the rest nodded in agreement.

After the voices dispersed Afonso heard Eulália haggle with Rosária, bartering eggs for the leftovers. Then, he listened as her determined footsteps echoed up the wooden stairs.

"Heard the news?"

"Hummm…"

"Fernando Cabeça-de-Aço has already packed his traps to help Salazar fight the guerrillas."

"What makes him so eager to die?" Afonso mumbled from beneath the covers.

"It's a man's duty to defend his people and his land. Always been, always will. I've told him you would be joining too." She stood by his bedside, hands on her hips.

"I can't be of help. I've never lifted a gun. Besides, it's not our land," Afonso lowered the covers, showing the white of his eyes and his fish-hook nose.

"Here's the chance to prove yourself. Stop complaining there's no decent work for a man in this dumb pit."

Outside, goat bells stirred the air.

"The crumbs Salazar pays wouldn't feed us long. I may even return a useless cripple." Afonso pulled the bed covers over his head again and lay deadly stiff.

Eulália's clogs tapped the wooden floor faster and faster.

"The little they pay will be far sweeter than the nothing you bring in now. As for becoming useless, better useless for a good reason than useless for no reason at all." She walked to the wooden shutters and swaying them open, rushed the day in. "A young man like you… tough bones and all, spending your living days in bed, buried in darkness. At least if you returned wounded you would gain the respect of our neighbours. War injuries are an honourable reason to sit idle. It would stop the serpent tongues in the village. They say you're a parasite and that I should fling the trap door open and drop you in the pen with the cow where you'd be put to better use. Another warm breath alongside the beast to heat the cool nights in the house. They don't say it to my face. I hear the whispers behind my back in the washing-pond, bad wind burning my ears. I see the weavings in their minds. If you want to clear the Almeida name you better hurry up and prove them wrong."

How could he ever clear his name now? After the excitement of their first kiss, Afonso had promised Eulália she would never have to worry about the future. He would provide for her. He would match the offerings of his love rival, Luis Couto. Afonso had promised and she had believed. Now, Luis Couto paraded his wealth refusing to hire him in the mill, on his fields, watching him rot. Afonso had no land to rest his hoe in, and they survived with a few vegetable beds in a plot Eulália inherited from her father.

"But…"

"No buts. Get off your idle one. If you aren't marching down the hill tomorrow I don't even want you in the pen." Eulália returned to his bedside and with a quick snap pulled the covers.

"Have mercy," he whined, curling up in a ball.

Afonso heard Eulália rush down the staircase, heard the metal blade of the hoe rasp against the cobblestone before she swung it over her shoulder.

"Otherwise I'll never look you in the face again," she yelled from underneath the balcony. The hammering of clogs faded as Eulália walked away to the field.

Afonso did not bother rising from under the covers to close the shutters. It was dark in his mind, and he fell asleep again despite the afternoon heat.

The noisy sweating of barbecued sardines dripping on hot embers woke Afonso. Their aroma watered his mouth. He peeked from beneath the covers. It was darker inside the room than outside and the stream's gentle murmur mingled with the sizzle of sardines. The sound tickled his throat. Through the balcony window he spotted occasional clouds and the bright path of the Milky Way. He called for Eulália. He heard a searing splash, then a pause. Eulália had stopped brushing olive oil on the sardines. After a moment the sizzle continued. She was ignoring him. He salivated. His stomach rumbled. The sizzle died.

It was an eternity before he heard water swishing. Tonight, Eulália had not even bothered to bring him food. His body shrunk, as if he was sinking. He panicked. His chest ached, pounded. He realised he was not breathing. He felt small. He was certain he could slip inside the skin of a fly. Eulália had closed the window of her heart. It was as if he was buried alive and he could feel the weight of her anger stomping on his face, pounding him down. And how could he blame her? Despite her silence, he had caught her glancing at the gold on Elvira Couto.

Afonso slowly pushed the bed covers away. He swung his legs over and sat on the edge of the bed, raking his new beard with knobby fingertips.

From the kitchen seeped the murmur of Eulália's voice praying her nightly rosary. Tonight, was she praying for herself alone? A pointed, solid object poked his buttocks. He stood and brushed his palm over the hay mattress, finding the small wooden crucifix from the wall in the hollow left by his body. He returned the crucifix to the nail and stared at the closed bedroom door. Gathering unknown courage from within a bottomless place, he lumbered to the door. It had been weeks since he had covered such distance. His legs trembled and threatened to collapse. He leaned against the doorframe. Lifted the doorstick. The door creaked.

On a stool, Eulália huddled around the embers in the hearth. She turned to face him. He walked to her side, staring while the incandescent glow tingled his face.

"Why do you want me marching to war, to death?"

"Dying isn't the only way to loose a loved one. I want you to do something, to leave that bed!"

Afonso thought of the domestic faces of war. Wills clashing under a slate roof. Walking toward her without the defence of armour. Her slashing words. Bleeding. Unprepared to defend himself because her eyes were the colour of buckwheat honey and he had imagined sweetness only.

"Why care what people think and not for my life?"

Eulália was about to respond. Then stopped. The lines on her face were carved deeper than he remembered. Her head slumped. She sadly stirred the embers, tightened the rosary in her hand.

"It's a good thing for a good man to do. And you'll touch the sea, go places."

Two sardines lay on a bed of corn bread next to the coals, staying warm. A sweet shiver travelled up his spine.

"I want us to touch the sea together." He placed his hand lightly on her shoulder. "Let's leave this skunk hole, Eulália, move to the coast. Our eyes will stretch, our dreams will sail, no longer corralled between mountains."

The gentle clinking of the cow's bell in the corral below spiralled through gaps in the wooden floor.

"Nothing fancy underneath our roof, but we're sheltered from the rain and we own a patch of land."

"We're penned like cattle, Eulália. It's a miserable life. That patch of land grows heartier stones than collards. What will our children eat? Look at the cow in the corral." Afonso lifted the trap door and a puff of warmth enveloped him. The pungent smell of fresh furze and urine doused the kitchen. He continued. "The cow lives in a pen hardly larger than her own body, she lives in darkness. She does it because she has a rope around her neck."

"We must live with what's given to us and find peace with the little we have." Eulália, rosary tangled on her knuckles, brought her hands to her chin. She mindlessly clenched the beads with her teeth.

Afonso walked to the narrow kitchen window. Lacing his hands behind his back, he gazed at the soft shapes in the moonlit yard. The crumbling walls of the empty hog pen. A hoe holding up the chicken coop door. The crooked, unhinged backyard gate. "That's easy if we are happy with what we have. I know the world has more to offer than Comba. I've seen it in my dreams."

His hunger had disappeared. The oak tree by the window rose above the house. Beneath, a blanket of acorns covered the ground. Acorns waiting for circumstance to drop rain and soften the soil so that sprouting arms finding a stronghold would thrive. Other acorns would roll into the slim stream meandering through the yard and be carried elsewhere.

Next door two kids bleated, tied to each other by a short rope. They pulled in opposite directions, attempting to reach grassy patches. Paralysed, they could not move. It was hopeless. Their legs folded, exhausted, and they lay down.

"I've failed you. I cannot give you anything I wanted to."

"No, you haven't failed me."

"I've seen you glancing at the gold on Elvira."

She did not respond.

He tasted emptiness in the silenced room. The stream of words exhausted. A dry, thick tongue. After a long while the chatter in his mind returned. He stared out the window, then at the trap door to the corral.

"I cannot bear the weight of the world on my shoulders. Why do I have to strike out alone and prove myself? Why do I have to carry us both on my back?"

The distinct snorting of a hog filled the silence. Eulália shifted on her stool.

"I've been carrying us," Eulália said, lifting one hand, showing him the white blisters on her sun-weathered hand. Afonso did not need to turn and look. She continued. "It's easier for a man to go out into the world and leave a mark, make things happen."

"Men pay a price. And in war, it's life!" Afonso cringed.

The snorting grew closer, louder.

"Do we have a new hog, Eulália?"

"No." She nodded surprised.

Afonso saw a hog's sinuous shadow sniffing the mint and parsley patch along the stone wall. Then, the hog waded into the stream to quench its thirst.

"Who would let their hog wander through the village at night? It's likely to raid people's gardens."

"Only gardens without proper gates or walls." Eulália said sharply. "Less feed Luis Couto has to grow to raise his hogs."

The hog ambled to the base of the oak tree and rubbed its skin on the trunk. Afonso watched its drool hang in thin suspended threads from its snout. The exhausted kids next door stood on their fours, craning their heads, looking on curiously. The hog settled under the oak tree and, with intermittent snorts, began gorging on the acorns.

Afonso stared at the moon floating in the sky, tangled among the oak branches by the kitchen window. In that motionless place, by that narrow window, he might stand until morning. And the moon, snagged branch to branch, would never be free.

Palms

Tomás leaned against the muddy wall of the trench furiously whittling a knotted tree branch. He paused, controlled his impatience, not wishing to carve the wrong groove. The knuckles of his hand were white, his fingers numb from the relentless work, the iced air.

He unwrapped his frozen fingers from the wood and warmed his hands under his armpits before firing random shots into the night. He waited for the enemy sentinel to respond dutifully. The shots echoed over the hill. Tomás sighed. One more hour of silence would now settle over the trenches.

Tomás sealed a rolled cigarette with his tongue and lit the smoke under his coat. As he returned the silver tobacco box to his breast pocket, he contemplated the bullet hole in the middle. His grandfather Manecas had slammed the box into his hand at the train station.

"Saved my life in the First," pointing to the box, "have a hunch it hasn't exhausted its luck yet."

Moments later the train whistle drowned his voice and the smoke forced his grandfather to reach for a handkerchief.

In the trench, the cigarette box lifted Tomás' spirits despite the fortune teller's sentence.

On his last day in town, Amélia had convinced Tomás to spend the day at the market.

He bought olives, she lupinis. They walked, arm in arm, around the crowded tents, he spitting black pits, she yellow skins, peeking at booths where merchants yelled out abundant praise for their wares, the louder the better. They were accosted by a rabbit vendor dangling the creature by its ears.

"Clean as a baby, no sores, no infections. My rabbits are the healthiest in the market," the vendor claimed as she spread the rabbit's legs a mere finger from his face.

"No doubt. But where I'm bound I'll find no use for rabbits," Tomás said gloomily.

"Take two then. I'll offer you a better price. There's nowhere one might be where the comfort of a pelt doesn't come in handy," she insisted, rubbing her hand along the rabbit's thick fur.

Tomás and Amélia pushed onward while the woman chased them a few paces down the lane.

"You'd be surprised how little care they need, how little space they take!" She pointed at crowded cages where the rabbits were squeezed. Amélia and Tomás hurried on, merging with the crowds.

Amélia suggested they visit the fortune-teller. They were engaged, and she wanted to prepare for how many children the future had planned for them, how long she must wait before his return.

The palm reader's tent was tucked away in the far corner, past the auction pens. With stripes of green, red and white, it was the most colourful in the market, and despite the stench, it displayed the longest queue on the grounds. Only the foozball tent, where the men gathered, rivalled its business.

In the queue, Tomás shifted from foot to foot, his heart in the foozball tent with his friends. He avoided the curious glances of women waiting their turn.

After hours in the braising heat, swatting flies and avoiding the swing of cattle's tails, a woman, handkerchief on her head matching the patterns on her tent, invited them in. As they stepped inside they were immediately blinded by the darkness.

"Crystal, card or palm? The fortune-teller asked before they had even sat down.

"Palms." Amélia said promptly.

"Left or right?"

"Does it make a difference?" Tomás asked, needing to assert his presence.

"Of course. The left palm shows your hereditary nature. The right, opens the door to the future, and it's more expensive to read of course."

Tomás did not like the fortune-teller's eyes. Black and glimmering, the eyes did not leave him at rest.

"Now, we must hurry. There's a long line of clients eager to learn their fortunes. Are we reading both yours and his?" She asked Amélia while lighting a candle. It was a woman's matter, and they conversed as if Tomás was absent.

"Both. But his hand first, please," Amélia requested.

The fortune-teller pulled Tomás' hand closer to the candle. The warmth of her hands shot an arrow up his spine. Tomás definitely disliked her piercing eyes.

"Goodness gracious! You show the palest lines North of the River Mondego. Bad sign. He suffers from weakness of decision, doesn't he?" She nodded to Amélia who nodded back in agreement. "I'm afraid I must double the fare. It's hard enough to read the paths of the future without having to cope with an uncooperative hand."

The fortune-teller searched the pockets of her apron and retrieved a monocle which she placed on her left eye. She peered over Tomás' hand, pressing it down flat. He could hear the occasional bellowing of cattle outside the tent protesting their way to the slaughter house. Her head shook sideways until she finally whistled in a grave tone.

"It's most discouraging. No sign of your future line."
Amélia tightened her grip on Tomás' other hand.

"And your life line," the fortune-teller continued, "shows a remarkably short length." Her fingertip followed a line curving around the base of the thumb.

Tomás heard Amélia's body swoon onto the ground next to him. He carried her outside for fresh air.

"Excuse me, but it's twenty thousand *réis*. I'm used to theatrics to avoid the price of truth." The fortune-teller had followed him outside. He emptied the silver from his pockets into her hands.

Tomás fanned his hat above Amélia's face until she recovered. Wide eyed, she stared at him as if he were already dead and yelled, "I can't wed a ghost!" Then Amélia stomped away, tossing her ring into the cattle pen.

After Tomás found the ring, he followed her toward the River Caima where he knew she would be sitting under the chestnut tree.

It had been some time since Tomás had finished his cigarette. The whittled wood had now taken on the shape of a hand. The fingers clearly defined, narrow fingernails in place, a sign of a calm disposition. Tomás began to carve his tomorrow. He fashioned the perfect lines from the hand pictured in the *Art of Palmistry* book he had picked up at the train station. He etched deeply, ensuring no possible misinterpretations about his future. The tip of his knife drew a line from the base of the palm following a straight course up, no cross lines representing serious obstacles or sharp changes. He traced a smooth and long lifeline placing a star in the

61

middle, a most fortunate sign. The heart line curving downwards from the base of the fingers ran over to the percussion without any branches or crosses to weaken its course. The wood grain even mimicked the prints on skin. Tomás sighed. He felt in complete control of his future.

An incandescent aurora illuminated the sky. Tomás raised the carved hand rotating it for a last inspection, ensuring no details were abandoned to chance. He slid his engagement ring down the wooden index finger, anticipating his promising new future. Tomás imagined Amélia's face smiling approvingly and could not wait to show her his masterpiece. Their life together would be idyllic now.

The sun rose, radiant and warm. Tomás filled his lungs with the hopefulness of the fresh day. Then fixing his eyes on the fading morning star, he placed his right hand over the machine gun's muzzle and fired a thunder of shells.

Forever Promises

Ti Clemente's thunderous voice, crisp and clear, shot through the night air. "I'll kill the bastard as soon as I get my hands on his chicken neck." Rumours claimed that Ti Clemente's voice, riding a full blown temper, travelled as far as Oliveira in the next valley.

Men, olive-oil lanterns in hand, searched every inch of ground. Sickles slashed arbutus bushes and the thump, thump of kicked stones tumbling down the slope intensified Lino's anxiety. Now and then the glare of a lantern ricocheted from an axe, and wounded his eyes. He lifted his body a notch further up the tree.

"Where're you hiding you son of a bitch? Come out. Be a man!" The blast of Ti Clemente's voice, carried by the wind, slapped the eucalyptus leaves. The leaves rattled in agreement.

Perched high in a eucalyptus, swaying with every gust of wind and shivering from the cold, Lino strengthened his grip on the branches, hoping to avert an argument with a sickle. He strained his eyes to foresee the future through the blinding curtain of night and fog. Lino was vigilantly waiting for amiable winds to carry him away, never to return.

After a weeklong drench had flooded the land, a drizzle persevered. A powerful scent of menthol exhaled from the trees and encircled Lino. His thoughts sailed far, distracting his ears from the approaching voices. He imagined the hills centuries ago, crowded in pine and oak, before the eucalyptus had arrived from the southern forests, during the Discoveries. Its fast roots and precocious maturity were rewarded by the mill with easy money. No one paid attention to the eucalyptus' insatiable thirst that turned the fresh water springs into trickles. "There is plenty of water in the sky," people said. No one seemed to worry. And judging by the last few days, the weather was proving them right.

An owl shrieked. It frightened Lino, momentarily upsetting his balance. An arm's length away, the bird perched on a branch observed him. The owl's slightly rotating head and intense, scrutinising eyes caused him further agitation. Lino shooed the bird away. The creature, a sharp seer in the night, glided away, piercing the curtain of blackness.

Lino's fingertips throbbed from the escape, the rush in darkness and the constant stumbles over deadfall. He rubbed his itchy hands on his drenched trousers. "Damn luck," thought Lino, "trust these hands to find every stinging nettle on this blind slope." The rain, swept by the wind, stung his face. Rain and disgrace poured down together. Rain had never been a favourable omen and he despised it more than ever.

The year it rained through the grape harvest and villagers cursed the weak wine—"There is more proof in milk than in this piss-coloured water,"—was the year Lino had truly noticed Amélia. First, he noticed her laughter. A laughter that stirred the dogs napping on the stone walls that braced the hill-terraces. It was not long before the song of her laughter spun his blood, leaving him dizzy and short of breath. Lino leaned against a grapevine.

Deep in the woods, he had attempted to emulate her laugh, a melody that fluttered up and down terraces, returning as fresh as before. The air, tripping in his throat, stumbled into the world as a limping cough. Lino bit his lips, well aware that Amélia would not be approved by his father Mário, "Working people who lose their tempers easily, not our stock." Confiding his feelings about Amélia would sentence him to a lecture on the bright future that lay ahead of him and the silliness of the idea, "You'll meet a fine woman, one who also takes to books." Amélia had never sat in a classroom. Her sweat had begun watering the fields while her cloth doll, clinging to her waist, still longed to play.

Wooden carts stationed by the trails glistened in the wet while bored bulls, cursing the attention, waved their tails at pesky mosquitoes. Amélia led the women flocking to the carts, wide baskets balanced on their crowns, the sway of their hips occasionally spilling a grape. A shout away, Ti Clemente and the men charged up and down ladders three times their height, their agile trunks disappearing among the dense foliage as if the upper half of their bodies had departed to the heavens leaving their dangling legs behind. And where land permitted standing and reaching for grapes, the women joined in the picking. Ti Clarissa and her repertoire of lyrics inspired the women in song.

Precious was the ground in this hilly country. A handful of soil pushed vines up granite columns, then curled them front-ward, fashioning lush parasols of leaves that shaded a spread of lettuce and kale covering the fields. Grapes hung from thin air like a Divine gift. Young mothers watched over their infants, sheltered beneath the cover of the fruit trees. A cry, intended to rouse a mother for a breast of reassurance, was more often met with a soother dipped in red wine and sprinkled with sugar, ensuring another uninterrupted stretch of labouring.

Amélia's strong, tanned body sparkled in the fields. Lino's eyes followed her through the weeklong harvest, blushing at a glimpse of her marble thighs as she bent to lift one more basket of grapes. His eyes touched skin even the summer sun had dared not. Lino's body tingled. He wiped the moisture on his brow.

A promise of gum engaged the young children, who chased grapes escaping from the swaying baskets and harvesting hands. "Every single pearl counts," encouraged Ti Clemente. Sharp eyes and swift hands engaged in a race against the sparrows. The sparrows chattered loudly as they plunged for a peck at the sweet pearls. Ti Clemente smiled when the children's smudged lips revealed the true destination of the grapes. The young ones forgot their task the moment the bulls stirred and the wheels creaked on stone, announcing a trip to the *lagares* to empty the carts. They gravitated to the carts in hope of a ride, perched on the back ledge, away from the driver's view.

As soon as the sun disappeared, Ti Clemente and the men climbed into *lagares*, their working day far from expired. Songs led stomping feet, up and down, down and up, nowhere to go. One hand anchored to a wooden bar for balance, another gripped a blood sausage while crushed grapes stained their skins. An occasional gulp of wine washed the grease down, "Fuel for the body," Ti Clemente claimed. Ti Clarissa and the women entered the *adega* to replenish trays of steaming corn bread and bowls of salty olives, then promptly returned to plucking that night's supper.

Boys, waiting for the ripeness of age, observed their fathers and uncles, drank in their seasoned words and sculpted their mannered poses, seeking desperate clues to the mystery of manhood. Manhood arrived as soon as their skinny stumps of flesh cleared the granite rim of the *lagares*. Until then they stomped in small wooden vats, their mouths opening wide to butter and sugar sandwiches, quick-crunching flashes of sweetness lighting their smile. As men's eyes blurred and words barely crawled out of their lips, Lino was happy to slip away unnoticed.

He sat on a boulder under the fig tree, between the kitchen and the fountain, sheltered from the drizzle, stealing a moment

66

away from the intrusive crowd. He tilted his head, his ear aimed at the commotion animating the kitchen. Amélia's voice easily rose above the others.

"I'll fetch more water. It's running low."

"What's the matter, girl? Taken a sudden interest in water, have you? Wanting to step in the rain after spending all day drenched in it. Don't lose sleep over water, there's plenty around this year," Ti Clarissa teased.

"I'll be right back," Amélia yelled as she guessed her way in the dark, a vessel on her head.

Lino moved closer to the trail in hope of a furtive brush of her skirt. He eagerly sat on the drenched grass.

"Can't stay long." Amélia stopped briefly, her leg touching his knee, her warm flesh searing through his pants, burning him.

"But the harvest is over tomorrow. When will I see you again?"

The following morning, dull terraces, bare of laughter and grapes, watched the carts carry Amélia away. Lino wished he had begged for a kiss.

An eroded trail, in winter a spontaneous brook avoided by the neighbouring goats, pulled Lino to Amélia's home every Sunday after the harvest. Sunday. School was out and the fields were at rest.

A Holy day. God demanded stillness from people. Just as well, when one's work was never done. Like the fellow Lino had studied in class, who wasted his life pushing a huge boulder up some mountain, only to have it roll back again. Up and down. Up and down. Nothing better to do. Nowhere to go. Lino pondered as he hopped from stone to stone, a book under his arm.

The day he stood outside Amélia's door, counting the layer upon layer of stones that fashioned the walls, studying the slated roof polished shiny and black by the rain, was the day that condemned him to the eucalyptus where he now dangled, shivering in the dark.

That Sunday, mesmerised by the patches of green moss that brightened the roof, Lino listened to the piercing wind hiss through the cracks, until the dog's bark rose above the gust and announced his presence. Ti Clemente, fresh from Mass, stepped out in a suit short at the cuffs, tight at the shoulders. His suit was evidently borrowed for the occasion of Lino's visit.

Ti Clemente's welcoming arms clasped Lino with a ripping noise of strained seams. Lino might have been entangled in that embrace indefinitely if it were not for his opportune cough.

"I better stop before I choke you boy. And you haven't done anything wrong yet." Ti Clemente laughed loudly.

Even before Lino muttered a greeting in response, he found himself sitting on the only chair in the house, across from Ti Clemente who sat on a stool. Lino listened for the third time to how happy everyone was to see him. Lino excused himself for wearing his wool coat in the house and reminded everyone of his frail health.

"Yeah! Should take better care of yourself. Should do some labouring in the fields. Impossible to work up a sweat flicking the pages in books. Reading never helped sharpening muscles… big eyes perhaps, but never man-size muscles."

Round loaves of corn bread, boiled potatoes, and two solitary chunks of *rojões* floating in lard arrived at the table. Lino, presented with the pork, accepted one, scooped a couple of potatoes, and poured a generous amount of lard over everything.

"Take that last, lonely piece of pork, Lino. It will go to waste. I've had my share of red meat in life, doctor's orders in regards to the uric…" he paused and scratched his head, attempting to remember his doctor's words, "…uric something." Then Ti Clemente continued, "Anyways, I'm forbidden to touch meat even with the tip of a driving-pole."

"Oh no, Ti Clemente, a king couldn't finish this plate. It's plenty," said Lino politely and to everyone's pleasure.

"Well, if that's the case, what the heck. Won't be killing me," he blessed himself just in case, "And if it ever did, I would be fortunate to die gratified. Better than wasting it on the dog and giving it undeserved satisfaction," concluded Ti Clemente snatching the last piece of pork while the younger children stared at the lard, their tongues running along shrivelled lips.

Lino and Ti Clemente sat face to face at the table, their elbows pinning down the red and white checkered plastic cover. Lino, spirit of a checker player, his impatient words leaping around, aimed for quick results. Ti Clemente, on the opposite side, paused at each sentence and contemplated every move, thinking ahead the way a chess player reflects into the future. The remainder of the family sat squeezed along a bench by the fire, a silent audience to the words and moves of the players. Amélia's mother interrupted merely to enquire about the enjoyment of her guest or to bring one more dusty bottle of red wine.

"So, what will you do once you become a doctor, young man?" That was Ti Clemente's traditional opening remark.

"I'll open a practice in Lisboa, save money, buy a red brick house, green grass at the front, like the English, you know, and a Ford of course," Lino gave his customary answer, his eyes fishing for a reaction from Amélia.

"Hope you don't forget the old friends back in the skunk hole!" Ti Clemente landed an expectant pat on Lino's shoulder. Lino, born in a golden cradle, was Ti Clemente's best prospect for a rescue from the bondage of the hoe.

"How could I ever forget the best fried pork in town," Lino said turning to Ti Clarissa, who feigned a grumble of disbelief at the compliment and immediately reminded him to leave room for sweet vermicelli, his favourite dessert.

Then Lino, a smile flashing his perfect teeth to Ti Clemente, added, "How could I ever forget the best conversation to be had in this valley. What do you say to a trip to the Capital in a black shiny Ford and a visit to the old Palace?"

"Oh! I couldn't possibly! I'll likely get sick. Never sat in one of those things myself, but I hear they move fast enough to miss the trees passing. Sure would be nice…"

"Never too late for an old dog to learn new tricks! That's what they say."

"Well, Lino, I'm not an educated man, can't tell the up or down of a book, but that doesn't mean I don't have thinking going on up here." He wiped his mouth on his sleeve, cuffs stained burgundy from the wine, before pointing at his balding head. "Young man, it was said of my great-grandfather, God let him rest in peace, that after his wake and when everyone had returned to their homes, two young scoundrels broke into the cellar intending to help their thirsty lips to his prized wine." He paused to measure up Lino, the clank, clank of his fork digging for a piece of pork trapped between his molars. "And that's when the old wooden floor collapsed and the coffin with my great-grandfather inside crushed them to death. What about that? People swore they found him with a grin on his face. This is History, young man, perhaps not the kind you learn in school."

That Sunday Ti Clemente carried on into the closing of the afternoon and Lino nodded at the trail of words without end. Ti Clemente chewed his food like the bulls in the pasture, serious and at leisure. Ti Clarissa suggested to him to hurry.

"Never had a stomach worry in all these years even though it makes Amélia's hair stand on end waiting to finish up the dishes," he explained to Lino.

Lino twisted in his chair, anticipating the traditional closure to the ceremonious meal, when Ti Clemente would excuse himself, "I wish I could spend the rest of the day in the company of such a learned young man, but my social obligations call me," and Ti Clemente would leave for the café to play cards with his comrades. Only then would everyone else scatter, leaving Amélia and Lino to sit by the fire and Ti Clarissa to chaperone as she mended the work clothes. Lino endured the tribulation of the journey and the discomfort of lunch for the magical moments that ensued. Soon after, Ti Clarissa, excusing herself, "Can't aim a thread through a needle's eye in this dimness," would leave to her room. Then Lino squeezed Amélia's hand tightly, sending sparks of fire up his spine.

That Sunday however was looking like a painful waste of an afternoon for Lino and Ti Clemente seemed determined to remain in his pasture. In a moment of desperation Lino heard himself ask for Amélia's hand in marriage.

Those magical words opened the gates to Amélia's castle and Ti Clemente called for a bottle of Port to celebrate the occasion. Ti Clarissa hurried back with one of the ten he guarded for each of his children.

"You are a fine young man with a favourable future, a little impulsive but with a healthy appetite for life. Amélia will be in good hands." They raised their glasses and toasted, "A promise is forever."

Lino returned home light as a bird hopping from stone to stone, swinging around grapevines, unaware of the downpour that had just begun. For the first time in his life he sang at the top of his lungs. When he arrived at the iron gates of his home, a taciturn father awaited him. News and crows flew swiftly and in straight lines.

"What's the matter with you? Are you dreaming? A Mateus never breaks his word. I hope your tongue was bloody certain. You'll honour the path you've carved." That was the last time he spoke to Lino.

The day of the wedding, Lino opened the window of his room inviting the drizzle to wash his face. The clouds hung low, almost pressing against his head. He moved slowly as if he were carrying the entire sky on his shoulders. He scratched his head, staring down, puzzled by the results of a long forgotten event, as if nature had played a prank during seeding. Lino dragged his bare feet around the perimeter of the room, shoulders arched, ploughing under the undesired crop.

He was still nauseated from the alcohol that had numbed the bachelor farewell. He had complied with the traditions, a song and raised glass. Another song…

In the distance, the toll of church bells hurried a clatter of clogs to morning Mass. The same echo had haunted Lino during Amélia's first and only visit to the Capital, where he was completing his studies. Through the noise of Amélia's clogs on the cobblestones, he had heard the chuckles of bystanders and towed her away to point out the street where one day they would build their home. He took her on the yellow street car, gave the man in the blue cap a tip to let her ring the bell. He sat her in a restaurant where strong curried flavours revolted her stomach, and then to the pictures where she screamed in panic when John Wayne pointed a gun at her. Amélia's solid body was sculpted by the harshness of the fields. Her scent, a blend of heath and manure, was that of a wild animal and contrasted with the softness of Lino's friends, their French perfumes, their sophisticated creams. After that visit, Lino's exams prevented him from finding spare time to visit Amélia in the valley.

Lino slid the dresser against the door, then the bed, and barricaded himself. When the time arrived to depart for church, he did not answer his father's fists on the door.

It was mid-afternoon when the villagers gathered outside Lino's window. His mother held the crowd at bay, suggesting that Lino had fainted from happiness. By the evening, the crowd grew restless and noisy and arguments shattered the glass in his window. Lino escaped through the attic, removed a tile, slid up to the roof and leaped off the end of the house onto the hillock. Lino scrambled through the arbutus bushes and the furze. He gesticulated his thoughts, giving them wings, and his arms waved in the air the way a field hand lifted fresh seeds to the wind for unpredictable gusts to scatter the future.

The Visible Horizon

Olive and cork trees will dot the landscape. We will not fan wind into this image. Instead, we will ignite a blazing sun, tinting the landscape crimson, blurring the horizon lines in the fashion of southern memories. The stunted yellow grass will rest still. We will prompt a raven to shriek and burst the silence. We will place three little shepherds on their backs under a holm oak, name them Lucia, Jacinta and Francisco. For the sake of pastoral, as well as literary coherence, let us surround them with a flock of sheep. The sheep are secondary to the story but may become a minor recurrent symbolic theme. We want subtlety of characterisation. We will portray the shepherds as poor, sharing among themselves olives and a loaf of rye bread.

The shepherds are young. Lucia, the eldest, scarcely stands above the horns of the oldest ram. They exhaust their days frolicking in the shade, inventing a thousand games, rolling on the acorn blanket strewn over the land. We might be tempted to introduce a landlord into the picture, decades of intemperance spilling his belly over white pants, but we risk succumbing to the traps of melodrama, or worse, cliché. So let us restrict ourselves to the shepherds and permit them to lead the story in a manner only children will.

The sun, high in the sky, forces every creature to the rescue of shade. The sheep congregate in small clusters under the holm oaks. The heat is unbearable and even flies nap on the branches of the olive trees. The children finish the rye bread and entertain themselves spitting the olive stones in long lazy blows at the surrounding sheep. From their water gourd, they fill up the remaining emptiness in their stomachs. The effort of breathing seems excessive under the sun's torrid weight. The children lie on their backs using the sheep for pillows. Through gaps in the foliage they stare at the sky and scrutinise the clouds for angels. This afternoon it is Lucia who recognises Archangel Gabriel in the heights. Once discovered, the angel requires little convincing for the children to engage him in conversation.

"Archangel Gabriel, why do you lay so still?"

The Archangel sighs, hardly stirring a leaf.

"Oh... children, I rest, tired of roaming the skies in search of a pure spirit willing to listen to Our Lady's word. Would you know of anyone?"

The children exchange puzzled glances and shrug. Then Francisco, the youngest, speaks.

"I'd try the green house over the hill where Ti Oslavo lives. Aunty says he's a saint of an old man."

Time passes.

The sun eases its glare on the land. The sheep begin to stir. The dangling of the sheep's bells hypnotises the landscape. The children remain beneath the umbrella of the holm oak. Time stops. The outside world does not interrupt the repetitive patterns of landscape and bells.

At day's close the children find themselves in total darkness and afraid to return home. They are afraid of the hollow darkness, its cold breath, so tangible they sense it against their cheeks. They believe they will be swallowed up the moment they step away from the holm oak's protective branches. They breathe safely against the aged face of its wrinkled trunk.

"We'll be safe under the holm oak, won't we? The giant's mouth cannot possibly squeeze under the tree, right?" asks little Francisco.

"That's right. It would pop his mouth the way a toothpick bursts a water-bladder," confirms Lucia. Jacinta and Francisco nervously laugh.

"The sheep will lie down to sleep and the monster will mistake them for tufts of grass," murmurs Jacinta.

They spot distant glimmers of light and believe they are the beast's thousand eyes. Hands pressed together, they fall to their knees. They mimic their parent's fervent devotion, praying in the midst of winter storms when the thunder rattles the pots on the stove and crashes mugs onto the wooden floor, "Hail Mary…". They have sinned and are being warned once more about their trespasses.

The children finish their prayers and bless themselves.

"We'll be alright," Lucia, wishing to cry herself, consoles the youngest. She remembers her aunt's words, her sharp finger writing the threat in air, "You must look after the little ones now that you're a big girl. Be sure nothing bad ever happens to them or else…"

"Our Lady will protect us from evil," Lucia speaks unnecessarily loud so as to believe her own words. She fits a child under each arm and this time does not stop them from rubbing their noses on her sleeves.

"How can you be so sure that Our Lady is protecting us? We're so little. She can hardly see us among the many of the world."

"Don't fear little ones. She's right here with us, up on that branch," Lucia points upwards into the hollow darkness. The little ones half raise their heads and squint to better follow the aim of her finger.

"I can't see Her," complains Jacinta.

"Neither can I."

"If you stop sobbing you just might. How can you expect to see the Lady through a curtain of tears?"

The youngsters wipe their eyes.

"I still can't see," complains Francisco.

"Of course not. Do you expect the Lady to show Herself to a dirty and snotty face?" Lucia admonishes.

The lights approach. There is a murmur. The little ones cry out that it is the monster's growling. They return to their crying, which intensifies Lucia's own fear.

"You must be quiet. The monster may find us. Besides, I need to hear what the Lady has to tell us."

Jacinta and Francisco are silent for a moment. They watch Lucia staring upward and nodding intermittently.

"What's She saying," Francisco pulls Lucia's arm.

"Don't interrupt. I'll tell you when the Lady's finished." Lucia sighs thankful for the silence and a tear of her own is freed to escape.

"You aren't looking up any longer. What did the Lady say?" Francisco tugs at her sleeve.

"Yes. Yes. Our Lady told me She's guiding the people She sent to help us. It won't be long now."

And Francisco smiles for the first time since the skies had darkened. He stares up the trunk to where the Lady had been and asks, "What does she look like?"

"She has the smoothest skin, the rosiest cheeks. Her smile beams beauty and peace."

"What was She wearing?"

"A deep blue cape sprinkled with radiance. From her clasped hands hung a rosary of crystals."

Jacinta and Francisco stare in awe at the crown of the tree

and the glimmering sky above. They forget the approaching murmur of the night monster.

"Children! Where are you burrowed?"

Their aunt's voice rises from the darkness.

"Aunt, Lucia spoke with the Lady! She spoke with the Lady," Francisco runs to their saviour's arms.

We will return the children safely home, lie them down in the warmth of their cots. We will whisper goodnight. We will draw a curtain of clouds over the night, blind the stars, silence the wind and the ravens. We will bring this story to a close.

We will be unable to prevent a pestilence, a bubonic fever, from spreading over the land. Many will perish, including two of the shepherds. In time we will also accept that we are unable to deter people from flocking to the holy holm oak, site of the miraculous apparitions, unable to deter those of deep religious faith from erecting a shrine. Our mothers, mostly, some years on foot, some years on knees, will embark on pilgrimages. Our lives will be touched, will change. The ravens shall return of their own will. The story will spread its wings and soar beyond the visible horizon of the sheep, cork and olive trees we created.

A Handful of Illusions

Me a devil? Never. The devil wouldn't dare to undertake this toil, these risks. I wear my fingertips down to chalkbone just to bring in clientele. Ah… not like a *padre*, having everything tailor-made, simply sliding into a robe and smudging sweet frankincense on the altar and having folks swarming in from their hives to his pews. *Padres* don't even bother with decent miracles. They were done so long ago, no one's going to question them now. What soul's alive to warrant it with their own eyes? Scribbled tales. A bunch of chicken scratches on paper standing as proof! If you ask me, an inspired skull with a fermented barrel full of imagination spilled a good yarn. I wish I were blessed with such luck. That kind of luck smells of lordly ways. In my case, I have it rougher than a toad's skin. Look at my hands. See, not like your Eminence's, smooth as candle wax. No. I must prove myself. There's been a trail of folk before me claiming to be saints, gods, diviners and Lord knows what else. But me… I don't claim fame or fortune. I ask to be left alone with enough bread to hush my belly.

Of course I haven't got any instruction, can't untangle the sense out of those feathered arabesques in books. What I know I learned from my ordinary eyes, swinging hoe, shoulder to shoulder with folk, listening to their aches, their longings. I have to prove to my folk that I can see into the past, predict the future, and deliver reasonable miracles. That much I owe them. They don't ask for much but they do like to see a wee thing or another out of the ordinary. Can't blame them. After all, they're paying bags of corn that cost them the salt of their brows to earn. Now, you want to blame me for using innocent tricks to help my craft a little? For God's sake, I'm flesh and bone. I have my limitations. Don't expect me to part waters or heal the blind. I borrow long-ago techniques to dispense a handful of illusions, see. It's day dreaming. Folk don't mind. Of course I don't tell them. The illusions are harmless. Do you remember the day you were told Saint Nicholas didn't exist? You'd rather have been kept in the belief of that pleasant dream, wouldn't you? Sure, not telling tales in the first place…

Let lightning strike me if I'm not speaking the truth, but in truth, since the birth of time, we've been deceiving each other a tad. Your Eminence's Holy Scripture even lends me reason. No, I'm not pretending to be Popier than the Pope. At the beginning Adam and Eve deceived one another. So I'm not undressing any secret. Perhaps there's more deceiving nowadays but it's born of the hunger of necessity. Everyone must eat, but few own the guns and the land to grow the corn. So I end up deceiving my own kind. The ones that also own nothing. I'm blessed with a bit more wit or perhaps just a thicker rib of wickedness. Anyway, some folk would rather be shod in dreams and fantasy than to walk barefoot through the bramble of life. If your Eminence doesn't mind me saying so and doesn't take offence, I dare say we're in the same line of business. We sell dreams, fantasies and hopes.

Don't be upset. Of course, I'm not trying to claim you don't know your gospel. I'm scarce in the learned ways of your Eminence, and I may have stepped into your territory, stolen a few too many souls from your flock. But on the honour of my dead mother I swear… alright I won't because it's sinful and we're in the House of the Lord. On the honour of my dead mother who was a saint, I then give you my Christian word that folk swarm to me of their free will. Well, whatever your Eminence says… if you say you're the one deciding who deserves to become a saint, that's fine by me too. Anyway, my mother was a saint to me.

It's a decent job of course, and a hundred times more honest than a money lender's or a landlord's. I shouldn't berate money lenders or landlords? They're most generous to the episcopate, are they? Vampires lounging on verandas, reclining under virtuous shade, counting gold coins, sipping mugs filled with drinks the colour of labourers' sweat. You smile. Don't think mine isn't a demanding craft. After the sun dies, my job goes on. Awake or asleep, my reputation rests on my devoted mind. And don't you think I live in the dreamy clouds. Yes, it's true some folk gather I'm no more than a charlatan selling lies, tricking souls. But to them I turn a deaf ear. They're jealous. I'm here simply to pluck up folk's courage in the face of daily tragedies; to dispense the hope folk hunger for because there isn't anyone else around to inspire faith any more. Every soul needs a little push to do what they must do. There's no muscle in the human body with the sheer guts of a heart. Folk swarm to my door and like to think I'm the reason their wishes come true. Let them believe. Nothing wrong with believing. No one is hurt. Folk have never trusted their own strengths. Instead, they journey to our land's four corners, seeking a saviour to avow their worth. They must hear it from another mouth, sometimes even from miraculous stones, before they'll believe it themselves. Folk believe in what they want to believe. They act on what they want to act on. I'm simply a way for these souls to wash their hands, see. In case life goes wrong, brings pain, as it always will, and when they fail they can blame me. I risk my neck everyday.

Of course I know I'm not in a place to negotiate. I don't pay watchdogs to guard my flock. You can snatch my sheep any time you please. Your dogs are fierce and inquisitive. They go for the neck and bite like vampires. I could even leave the village if your Eminence thinks it advisable.

Certainly a good confession never hurt anyone. A proper and respectable household begs regular dusting to please the sight. Pity one needs to repeat it over and over. Dust is the kind of bother that grows out of air. One never learns! Dust insists on returning. But a proper wipe has never failed to give a new appearance to things, that's true.

Why would you want me to spill the secrets of my craft? I may be lay but I'm not naive. You don't ask a baker to hand over her oven or a troubadour to surrender his lute. Would you renounce your cathedral? But I may make an exception, if it may be looked upon favourably for my case. I don't suppose there would be a jug of burgundy and a morsel of smoked ham to help grease my words. My tongue dries out at the thought of confession. The holy wine will be fine. God bless you!

Hmmm… Ahhh! Yes, back to the secrets of my craft. When business is slow I do remind the living about the world of the spirits by sewing toad's mouths and planting the creatures on folk's doorsteps. Two weeks of this and folks swarm to my door. Then I prescribe a cleansing brew of milk thistle followed by a string of prayers, sung on their knees, counter clockwise around the yard. Folk believe they must suffer before they're given what they've long deserved. I must thank your Eminence for this creed. And, very important, I always prescribe the burning of a dozen candles. I sell them at the door.

I'm very sorry, your Eminence, I never imagined it was hurting church business. It's a nice slice of the pie now that I think of it. Uuuhhhhh… You don't understaaand me? Taasty morrrsel…

Forgive my ravenous manners, will you? But your Eminence has kept me for two moons on bread and water. I'm reeaady for another jug of that divine grape juice.

Surely my craft demands the ears of an owl and the eyes of an eagle. You'd be surprised how much you find about a person by observing the rags on their bodies, the adornments they wear or don't, weighing the timbre beneath each word. Just as important as planting my youngest in my kitchen, pretending to play, talking to them, digging up relevant information from their past. Later, I'll impress them right off the bat wing with intimate gems about their lives. Folk forget how much of themselves they bare to each other in their mundane lives. That's why I never attend to a soul when they first seek me. It takes time for a mole to dig a maze of connections.

True. Mostly women seek my remedies for life's burdens. Matters of love and children, for those are the ingredients of a woman's life. When I see them struggling up the trail, a child in each arm, two clinging to their skirts, it's a sure bet they come for a remedy to stop bearing. I offer them a concoction my grandmother passed on to me. Begin by placing a handful of corn silk, having previously been chewed by an ass, into a glass container. Be sure to add three strings of the ass' tail hair. Tie them in a circle. Next, brew an infusion of pennyroyal. Watch it steep. Sprinkle a pinch of brewers yeast. Add everything to the corn silk. Stir well. Strain the liquid. Drink the concoction in seven separate sips, and every time a cock crows. Between sips sing, "Spit of ass trapped in glass stop my belly from swellin'." But if I happen to have sea sponges from Hell's Mouth Bay, soaked in lemon juice, I offer them those. I just can't keep them on hand, such is demand. They never fail me. And then there is the magic to force one's husband to be faithful. A woman must fill a thimble with the marrow of a black dog and place it in a red velvet pouch. Next she must bury the pouch in the heart of the straw mattress so the man doesn't notice the thimble in his sleep. Throughout the week, before bed, she must give him drinks of barley with plenty of cinnamon and clove, and must sleep unclad, moving as close to his body as she can bear, so to pass the man her desire through her perspiration. If the precious detail of this prescription is faithfully obeyed, success is destined.

Forgive my frankness, your Eminence, but pacing in circles treads on my nerves. If you sat down I could brew camomile flowers with a spoonful of wild honey and a sprinkle of auspicious words. Not! I'm trying to help! It's a habit. I'll do whatever your Eminence wants me to do. I'll wash your Eminence's feet with my hair if need be. I'll go to Mass daily if that helps. I'll chant the rosary, and I'll be the most pious of the congregation.

With all due respect, what does your Eminence mean with me regretfully having to stand as an example? To get rid of me won't serve any good. As soon as my tongue sticks out to the world and my legs dangle like an angel's... Yes, naturally not like an angel. Anyways, as soon as I'm cold under the full moon, another soul will step in to fill my shoes. It's in folk's blood, believe me. On the other hand, if you let me look after my own affairs, we might reach a pleasant little agreement that will leave us both singing and maybe we could even shake hands? I will even move to the outskirts of town. You stay on your side of the fence and I on mine. I don't even expect much to live on. You can keep the sunny side of the bargain. You reckon I have knack for words and negotiate like the devil? I don't suppose that's praise.

Chestnut Tree

Tomás stepped off the bus into a gust of wind. Seven years of memory rekindled with the rich fragrance of burgundy grapes. He raised his arms, stretching his bones from the journey, inhaled a long gulp of air, and filled his chest with the luscious green of the fields. Feet sunk into the roadside grass, his eyes meandered over the terraces. His tongue smacked against the sky of his mouth in a loud crack. Home. Tomás dried a tear with his jacket sleeve.

Grapes dangled in a nearby vineyard. Tomás reached for a glowing handful and crossed the road into the shade. He leaned on a walnut tree and scrutinised the landscape. Distant bodies slithered in and out of vines, harvesting grapes. A string of women, baskets on their crowns, filled wooden carts. Tomás leisurely savoured each grape, spitting the seeds in a long arc across the dusty road. The wind carried the songs of labourers and leaves spiralled in midair. His gaze followed a lone leaf upwards until it disappeared against the hill-terraces tinged crimson by the ripe vineyards.

Tomás slowly found his way through the fields. The people, not recognising him behind the scarred face and the deep African tan, greeted him politely and resumed their labour. Tomás smiled, imagining their surprised faces when he announced himself in Ti Anastácio's *adega.*

Tomás located the meandering trail that led down to his land next to the River Caima. The fields appeared carefully tended, the grass trimmed short by pasturing cattle. Sweet Amélia had been attending to the land. The orchard stood tall and mature now. Tomás cleared a bend in the trail and his legs weakened. He rested on a boulder, staring in disbelief. In place of the chestnut tree, provider of indefatigable shade, stood a rotten stump. At the River Caima's edge, the abandoned water mill kneeled, decomposing at the hands of merciless winters. Why had Amélia allowed the chestnut to be cut down?

Under its wide and ragged leaves, they had stolen their first moonlight kiss. And years later, on his last day in the village, Tomás had sat under the chestnut tree promising Amélia that he would return soon and be a father to the child in her belly. Pointing to an apple sapling in their orchard, he had reassured her, "I will return in time to harvest the first Golden Delicious for our child. The fortune-teller's words are nonsense."

Tomás walked to the mature apple tree and stretching on his toes picked two Golden Delicious. He mindfully guarded the apples in his jacket.

A few more steps along the trail Tomás discovered that Ti Anastácio's *adega* had vanished. He cursed the blue-tiled monstrosity that had replaced the old quaint *adega* and the drapes of vines that had brightened it. His eyes inched up the terraced village afraid of the changes in his path.

Tomás shivered.

In the torrid humidity of the makeshift bamboo cage, Tomás had killed time telling his cellmates about the valley of his childhood. Fearful of a land that whispered sounds he did not recognise, threw smells he cringed at, and delivered food he could not digest, Tomás had sheltered himself in memory. The stories invited his cellmates into every home of the village, sat them in Ti Anastácio's *adega* where he introduced them to Quim, the best quadrille player. Quim and Tomás had devised secret hand signals and there was not a soul who could beat them at cards. In the tavern the men listened to soccer matches blaring from the only radio in the village. On a Sunday, every man could be found at Ti Anastácio's door. Some stayed out on the sunny benches resting their bodies from six days of toil in the fields; others threw iron in quoit games. Tempers were high especially when money, not merely the buttons off their shirts, was at stake. Tomás maintained his distance from quoit games where crafty tactics were no match for a steady hand and perfect aim. Hands busy with quoit or quadrille, everyone listened to the soccer match on the radio, contented to interrupt their play to cheer or curse the goals.

Tomás had shared domestic reveries with his cellmates, inviting them to turn his old plain shack of piled stones into a lime-washed palace with geraniums in the windowsills. Precisely what Amélia had always desired. Tomás promised to find each of his mates a girl at the corn husking festival, devising a way to slip into their pockets the rare maroon corn ears that warranted rounds of kissing and hugging.

In the sizzling African heat, keeping a vigilant eye alert for deadly spiders, Tomás had spun tales of home, promising his cell mates a round of *vinho verde* at Ti Anastácio's place the day they returned safely to their motherland. By the end he mostly talked to himself, reliving his memory while José came in and out of a tsetse-sentenced sleep. An entire battalion had slowly evaporated like puddles of hope trapped under the sun. Malaria, tsetse, insolation, bilharzia or snakes. Snakes searched for the warmth of human bodies in the cool of the night. A soldier was merely a turn away from death. Tomás had never slept so close to another man.

At night, far more annoying than the baying of Ti Anastácio's pitiful watch dog, the howls of the hyenas crashed into his nightmares. Tomás had promised never again to shower the dog with stones.

His heart tight as a fist, Tomás spotted his old house fresh and white against the surrounding greenery. Geraniums in clay vases smiled from the windowsill. He did not know how long he had been staring at the house when down the stone-paved trail came a band of children racing rusty bicycle rims, a short stick steering the fast moving vehicle of their fantasies. At their age, Tomás had dreamed of the day he would link the discarded parts into a bicycle.

Tomás stopped the children.

"Any of you a Faria kid?" He looked into their eyes for a resemblance of himself.

"No, sir."

"Can you point me to Tomás Faria's house?" He smiled.

"Never heard of him," one said nodding his head in certainty.

Tomás clutched the apples in his pockets, kicked a stone on the trail. The child continued.

"The last Faria I know of was Ti Ezequiel Faria and he died last year. Left no children to this world. That's what I heard my mother say," the child rolled snot between his fingers and flicked it away.

Tomás imagined his father resting in his coffin, his inseparable crimson handkerchief tucked in his Sunday suit breast pocket. He was unable to see his father's eyes. What would they have spoken about on his death bed?

"Who lives in the beautiful lime-washed house?"

"I do with mother, father and my older sister Rosa."

Tomás traced his footsteps back to the river trail and paced back and forth along the shore, collecting grey flat pebbles. With both pockets filled, he skipped them fiercely across the water surface. The pebbles drowned in the fast current. The river continued on. His thoughts remained trapped in the vortex of an eddy.

A cacophony of feminine voices approached. Tomás retreated to the shadow of a fig tree. A file of women, towers of laundry balanced on their heads, arrived at the river's edge. They knelt on the grassy shore, rasping colourful fabric against worn granite slabs.

"Heard of the stranger walking through town this morning?" a woman finally asked while rinsing long johns, the trapped air fluffing them up at the crotch.

"Doesn't take much to fill that crotch!" a young woman teased, and for her response received a splatter of water.

"People are saying he's the spitting image of Tomás Faria's ghost!"

"Don't go 'round spreading rumours, creature. You'll bring his spirit back from where it rests in peace." She raised both hands to the sky.

"As if it wasn't enough Calvary what poor Amélia lived through. Imagine the disgrace of facing the ghost of your dead fiancé after remaking your life with a good man."

"There would be no worse tragedy than to bring the man back. Stale water lost under the bridge," agreed the first woman.

Their talk veered to their children, the wine crop, the weather, until the words were replaced by the rhythmical slap of clothes on water.

Tomás walked in a daze around the fields until the sun disappeared, and he found himself in Ti Anastácio's tavern.

In a dim corner, three young men he did not recognise stared at a television. Tomás walked to the counter and ordered a bottle of fresh *vinho novo.*

"Where's the old bugger, Ti Anastácio?" Tomás forced a cheerful tone to the question.

"Been gone a long time. Died of heartbreak shortly after losing this place at cards," the man at the counter said giving another turn to his rolled sleeves, coughing and clearing his phlegm onto the tile floor.

"I see. Who runs this place, now?"

"Quim Lesto. Missed him by a shadow," he said, pouring from high, the first glass full. The top foamed.

At that moment Tomás hated Quim, hated the plastic formica that replaced the marble counter, hated the glossy tile that replaced the stone floor.

"I'm looking for an old friend of a friend. Where could I find the Farias?" Tomás tapped his nails on the counter and glanced at the TV screen.

"Any of you heard of any Farias in this town?" the man yelled to the young men in the corner.

They shook their heads without looking away from the television.

"Looks like we can't help you here," the man said with a grin and another cough.

"We could use another pair of hands for a game of quadrille, though!" one young man said, keeping his eyes on the screen.

"Thanks but don't know how," Tomás said half biting his lip.

He finished his bottle in silence.

Tomás leaned against the abandoned wall of the water-mill, cursing the valley nights, their humid chill. He tucked his shirttail into his trousers, a futile attempt to prevent the fall's frosty air from biting through to the bone. Now and then he heard the crackling of twigs.

paulo da costa

An owl, perched on a nearby apple branch, hooted insistently. Believing in bad omens, Tomás shivered. In the distance, smoke spiralling from chimneys dissipated into the stars. He smelled the comfort of wood burning.

Tomás stiffened at the sight of two shining-dagger eyes behind the bramble. So low to the ground, he was certain they were a beast's. He pretended to ignore the eyes, then, with a sigh of relief he recognised Ti Anastácio's dog.

"Come on over old bugger. It'll be warmer wrapped around each other." The dog, arthritic and old, his silvery fur coat shedding, curled at his feet.

Tomás begged the dog's forgiveness for all the stones he had ever thrown, until his slurred and exhausted words stumbled in the darkness and silenced him.

In his drowsiness Tomás thought he heard a cough, muffled. The dog growled faintly. Tomás succumbed to tiredness and slipped into a dream where an African snake finally joined him in sleep, slithering up his back, coiling around his neck. The pungent odour of *vinho novo* flooded his nostrils, and the cold snake tightened its grip on his neck. Tomás had difficulty breathing and woke up with his chest exploding. A breath away from his face, hands tightening around his neck, Tomás saw the bloodshot eyes of a man leaning over him.

"Damn ghost. Why did you come back to haunt us?"

The dog bayed. Tomás did not resist. He hoped he wore a peaceful expression on his face. His chest ripped at the seams. His vision rapidly muddled. Darkness swallowed him. Tomás heard a woman's voice in the distance as he floated skyward. The man released his grip on Tomás' neck. Tomás lay gasping for air, not daring to open his eyes. He thought he heard a muffled sob.

Tomás recognised Quim half-hiding his face in his large knobby hands. Out of focus, a few paces behind him, stood Amélia. The dog growled, bared its teeth. Tomás broke out in a cough, spat out blood. He drew a deep breath. Amélia slowly

91

came into focus. A terrible ache clutched his heart.

"Amélia dear, you glow as brightly as the day I left," Tomás whispered. He recognised the rose patterned maternity dress, her bulging belly. Tomás wondered if he had ever left.

"I have to kill you!" Quim picked up a stone and raised his fist.

Amélia walked over to Quim, opened his fingers and embraced him. "Stop it, Quim. We've spent the day arguing about this already." The stone dropped on the dog. The dog yelped.

Quim stomped away snarling and crushing the small bushes in his way.

Amélia stood motionless staring at Tomás. Their eyes roamed the absent years, discovering new scars, new folds on their faces. Nearby, Quim's wolf-like bellow accompanied the sound of river boulders crashing, shattering the air. It reminded Tomás of grenades falling, and he thought he could see sparks. The dog snuggled closer to Tomás.

"I just wanted to see you Amélia. He can kill me now."

"Don't speak nonsense, Tomás."

Amélia kneeled beside Tomás. She touched Tomás' wooden hand, traced his gold band, then turned to the chestnut stump glowing under the moon's eye.

"The fortune lines on my new hand are auspicious, Amélia."

"I want you to meet Rosa, your daughter," she said, turning toward him again.

"Who would I be to her? A stranger?"

Tomás searched his pockets.

"I suppose I would like to give her this," Tomás said, holding a Golden Delicious apple in his palm.

Amélia's body shuddered. He remembered it shuddering when he had walked away to Africa.

"Yes, you must give Rosa the apple."

The boulders stopped crashing. There was silence. The creaking of small twigs announced Quim's return. Amélia stood up and waited. She hurled her arm around his waist and spoke. "The past doesn't need to be buried, Quim. We can bridge it. Tomás can move in with us for a while. Help you in the tavern, help me in the fields. Then we'll see."

"I don't need any help. This scoundrel will never sleep under my roof," Quim said and stepped away from Amélia.

"You must mean my roof, my house, only later your roof too. So, I decide. Not you. You can both live in the tumbledown walls of the late Ti Faria then. Fix it up together. Good medicine to get along. You were best friends weren't you?"

"What will the village think if we were to all live together?"

"It's what we think that matters. The village will live with what we choose."

"Do you love him?" Quim looked away as if fearing the answer.

Amélia looked into Tomás' eyes, scrutinised his face.

"I don't know. I did love him, but rivers change their course. We aren't the same people. I don't know him any more."

The frost glimmered on the blades of grass. An owl flew serenely above them and perched on a nearby apple tree. The smell of wood burning reminded them of the night's cold teeth sinking through their skin.

"Where would he sleep?" Quim crossed his arms over his chest.

"You'll share our room with Tomás. I'll move into the children's." Both men's eyes widened and they stared at each other incredulous.

In the uncomfortable silence Quim shuffled his feet while Tomás rubbed the dog's scruff.

"Well, maybe you can teach me some new tricks at cards and we can team up against the new young blood at the tavern? Just like old times!" suggested Tomás.

Quim looked up at the sky and rubbed his chin thoughtfully. Slowly, he lowered his eyes and met Tomás'.

"We were the best, weren't we?" Quim smiled and remembered the times he and Tomás were inseparable. "But how could you possibly play with one hand?" he added puzzled.

"Don't underestimate me. There is always a way." He winked at Quim, pointing out the carved notches on his wooden hand where cards would rest. Both men laughed.

Amélia extended a hand to Tomás. He shivered. He coughed. His teeth rattled.

"Come and join us for a hot bowl of *caldo verde*."

Tomás felt a tear roll down his face. Amélia had remembered his favourite kale soup.

"Can the dog live with us?"

Amélia and Quim stared at the dog curled at Tomás' feet.

"Why not? The creature hangs around the tavern all day anyway," Quim said.

"Maybe we can even teach him how to bark out our opponents' cards?"

Everyone laughed.

"Let's go before you die of pneumonia." Quim took his coat off and wrapped it around Tomás

Braced between their arms Tomás rose to his feet. The smell of wood burning filled his lungs. Under the moon's glow he noticed new shoots rising from the chestnut stump. Tomás felt the comfort of his arms entwined around the warm bodies and drew Quim and Amélia closer. They walked together across the fields, towards the light streaming through the window.

A Breath Of Memory

Florindo Ramos loved trees since one turbulent winter day when, as a limber boy, hopping from stone to stone on the edge of the River Caima, he had suddenly slipped, plunging into the careening current. "I'd have drowned if it hadn't been for my Ginkgo, growing by the lip of the river," Florindo told the children gathered around him after school, listening to his tales. Lovingly, he stroked the glossy green leaves of the saplings growing under the canopy of the mother Ginkgo. "I helplessly flapped my arms, sinking quickly. But my Ginkgo leaned almost out of the ground," he pointed to her exposed roots which resembled legs, "and she swept her arms into the waters to save me." Florindo tenderly kissed the reddish tree bark while leaves stirred shyly above the children's heads.

Following that miracle, in the evenings after his father retired to bed to say the rosary and to dream of sacred mysteries, Florindo climbed out of his window to the Ginkgo. He slept curled around the tree's feet as the River Caima flowed and gurgled at his toes. His palm on the trunk, he felt the Ginkgo's pulsating sap pulling nourishment from deep inside the earth.

Awakened in the morning by the yellow warblers' perfect

95

songs, Florindo rose and, stretching his arms, brought the Ginkgo's flowering buds to his nostrils, filling his lungs with the pungent odour. He yawned and rubbed her leaves between his fingers to freshen his skin. The tree breathed out, Florindo breathed in. He breathed out, the Ginkgo breathed in. An enriching and nourishing conversation.

Ti Clemente and many of the other village people disdained Florindo Ramos' apparently useless life. While Ti Clemente headed for the fields with the sunrise and toiled until the last crumbs of light fell from the sky, Florindo sat under the shade of his Ginkgo surveying the world.

"Should put his chit-chat rigmarole to good use behind the ploughing bulls, convincing the beasts to budge," Ti Clemente snorted under his breath, leading a team of bulls to the field with the prick of his driving pole.

"But he's in love with his maidenhair tree," excused Ti Clarissa, walking behind Ti Clemente. From time to time she secretly brought corn bread to Florindo. "He's happier than any of us. See the attention he pays her," she pointed at Florindo brushing the Ginkgo's trunk with a corn broom.

Florindo did not respond to the swing of Ti Clemente's axe-like tongue. He finished grooming his Ginkgo and then sought solace from the day's heat beneath his tree while her fan-shaped leaves gently swayed and stirred a breeze, cooling the air.

Nose to the grass, sprawled under the Ginkgo, Florindo awoke one afternoon contemplating no particular thought. He watched a bumble bee collecting pollen when suddenly, the crystalline words of his deceased grandmother flooded his mind. Florindo slowly remembered the days they had strolled together across cornfields, along the River Caima, picking bouquets of wild violets from the southern slopes. "Come closer. Bathe in their perfume," his grandmother had whispered, bringing the bouquet closer to his nostrils. The delicate petals had tickled his nose. Florindo gradually realised that the same air that had dwelled in the field and in his grandmother's lungs, now stirred in his chest and brought him pictures of the past. He smiled and clacked his tongue.

"Memory is breath," he exclaimed aloud and placed a blade of grass between his thumbs, blowing a long shrill note. Florindo expanded his lungs with air, thinking how the moment lungs emptied, life ceased. People stopped remembering; remembering who they were, remembering the habitual traps of past deeds. Memory disappeared on the wings of the last breath and there was nothing, only the vacuum of death.

Years later, in a city hospital, visiting his father, Florindo watched a faint tube filling his father with forgetfulness, edging him towards death. He ran his fingers along the tube entering his father's nose, examined the bottles pumping air into his body to keep him alive, and realised his father was on a mistaken path to regain health.

"You're feeding him lifeless, bottled air," he complained to the doctor. "My father must return home. He must lay among his family, sharing the air we breathe to remind him of who he is, where he comes from!"

The doctor stared at Florindo's reddish face and the bits of scattered leaves nesting in his locks. The smell of fresh grass permeated the air.

"I understand how disconcerting it must feel," the doctor said, patting Florindo's shoulder, offering him a glass of water and a fluorescent pill. But Florindo's eyes were mesmerised by the large poster of a human lung hanging on the wall. He walked closer to the picture and with his nail smoothed and smoothed out the paper's creases.

In the picture, the lungs resembled the tips of tree branches, "It's here the air whispers in and out," Florindo said excitedly to the doctor. It was as if people carried a miniature forest inside their chests. "Huuummm... the alveoli," nodded the doctor. He burst out laughing and Florindo ran, short-winded from the stagnant air of the hospital.

That evening, the Ginkgo nestled Florindo in her branches, rocking him back and forth as he cried himself to sleep. In Florindo's dreams the Ginkgo whispered that he must grind her leaves, mix them in water and offer it as a drink to his father. "It'll open the air flow to his heart. His memory will improve," the Ginkgo insisted in the assured voice of the oldest lineage of trees on earth, survivors of countless trials.

With no sign of a breeze, and as if nudged, Florindo awoke from his dream stretched out on the ground. The Ginkgo leaves rattled frenetically. Florindo hurried. He collected a handful of her leaves and ground them with a stone on a flat smooth rock. Then he ran the distance back to the city and slipped into his father's hospital room with the Ginkgo paste in his pouch. He opened the window in the room and spent the remainder of the night moistening his father's lips with the concoction.

In the morning, when his father had regained consciousness, the doctor sent him home, "Spontaneous remission," he concluded, scribbling in his medical charts.

Dark clouds gathered over Vale D'Água Amargurada when Florindo returned with his father. The pines and oaks brandished their branches. A wind lifted clouds of dust. A cold hiss swept across the fields. In the schoolyard a group of children played, galloping stick horses, sword fighting in a battle of knights. Leaves rattled incessantly like grinding teeth as lightning tore the sky to rags. A tree creaked and crashed down on the sawmill. Drops began to fall.

Florindo ran to his tree. Tearlike sap dripped from a broken limb on the Ginkgo while at her feet, her crop of saplings had been ripped up and torn. "I see you tried to push away the thoughtless plunderers," Florindo whispered, placing his face on her moist trunk, running his hand down her back. Tearing his shirt in strips, he bandaged her limb and carefully improvised a sling.

Florindo felt the earth tremble as the pitchfork of lightning bolts sank into the ground. The River Caima rushed, sparked by the lightning that travelled through its veins. The hairs on Florindo's neck stood up. Hurriedly, he gathered armfuls of leaves and buried the saplings. Then he walked to the schoolyard and collected the children's abandoned swords. Under the Ginkgo he thrust them through the leaves and into the ground where they rose like beautiful crosses. "You must be buried in the place you were born," Florindo solemnly said and played mournful songs on his harmonica until the rain stopped.

After the deluge, the children tentatively stopped at Florindo's Ginkgo on their way home from school, books tucked under their arms.

"Florindo, *Professor* Manecas says we should be doing our homework rather than wasting our time talking to you," said Bonifácio Careta, who was the most sceptical of the bunch and always stood, afraid to dirty his yellow knickers.

Florindo sighed to the Ginkgo. Then he replied.

"Come closer." He motioned them, "I'll tell you a secret." The children huddled around him like fiddlehead ferns. "A tree grows branches in many different directions," Florindo said, lifting his thumb upward to the Ginkgo. "If you follow the aim of each branch you'll see many different things. Things you otherwise might not notice."

The children looked upwards, each finding a branch to follow. "There's a pigeon's nest on the church steeple!" "And a rabbit's den across the river!" "A horse cloud!"

Florindo nodded and proceeded.

"*Professor* Manecas teaches you that knowledge is in books. But remember, books are made of trees." The children gaped at their books, then at the Ginkgo. Florindo continued. "Maybe those who write books think they concoct things in their minds, but they are fools. The knowledge was already there waiting to be remembered and inked."

Florindo wetted his index finger and flipped open a school book. He rubbed a single book leaf between his fingers. The paper crinkled. "That's very thin knowledge compared to the trunk of a tree," Florindo said and then made the ginkgo leaf that dangled from the corner of his mouth twirl along his smile with the movement of his lips. "Sit under a tree long enough and you will also know things," Florindo concluded and took up his harmonica as a light drizzle began.

The village children eagerly ran to visit Florindo after school and they listened to the wondrous stories that shed light on the workings of the world. His stories were as sweet as the wild honey that dripped from the beehive in the Ginkgo's upper branches, and as tart as a ripe olive.

"Florindo, don't put monkey ideas in their heads," Ti Clemente yelled from afar, half-chuckling, as he walked back from the fields with a bundle of grass on his head, destined for the corrals.

Florindo's concepts had been called "monkey ideas" since he told the children that people descended from trees. Florindo walked to the lumber camp at the edge of the village and gathered the children around a stump that was as wide as a table top. He placed his open palm on the stump, next to the rings on the wood, and showed the children that people and trees were cousins. The awed children released a collective whistle. The resemblance of the contour lines on the dead tree and their own fingertips was undeniable. "The trees left their imprint on our hands from the time we dangled from their branches," said Florindo. A story that fell from grace when it reached Padre Lucas' ears during catechism and required much holy water to dilute its heretic effect.

The children continued to flock to Florindo's presence. Florindo not only told stories, but also gave his full attention to their own stories. He listened to shy Alzira as she remembered being a bullfighter, describing in minute detail her foot dance in front of the bull, the colourful *bandarilhas* in her hands, the inciting sound of the trumpet.

Florindo believed that traces of past lives lingered in children's bodies. But as they aged, thoughts of the present left no room for lives past.

Senhor Mário Mateus peered from his window and waited for the children to be called home for supper. Then, in the company of his faithful umbrella, and ensuring no one noticed the detour from his daily stroll in the hills, he stopped by Florindo and his Ginkgo tree.

"Florindo, let's say you knew of someone in need of advice on how to clear the nightmares out of a haunted mansion. What would you suggest?" Senhor Mário Mateus shuffled his feet, staring at the sky.

Believing every house carried remnants of ancestral presence, Florindo did not believe in haunted houses.

"A house overburdened with the breath of the dead is lopsided," Florindo told Senhor Mário, and pointed at the roof of his mansion, sagging under the load of the years. "To balance, open the mansion's glassy eyes to a sunny day and invite children's laughter to share your dwelling. Children's play, as they run to and fro, keeps the air moving."

"That's a rather complicated solution. Do you have anything simpler?" Senhor Mário retorted. Florindo ignored his comment and continued.

"A well-aired house restores balance."

Senhor Mário Mateus scratched the ground with the tip of his umbrella and muttered indiscernible sounds before staring at the sky again.

"And what about ridding ancestral ghosts in just one bedroom then?" Senhor Mário Mateus said as he straightened the rose in his lapel.

"Ghosts want to be heard," Florindo said. "Ancestors' thoughts—trapped in the wall tapestries or clinging to the dust on yellowed photographs—are as essential as bread and water to a joyous home." Florindo paused and noticed Senhor Mário's hands, his knuckles white from clenching his umbrella. "Sometimes the dead require the hands of the living to repair the wrongs they rendered in their lives. Once we listen and cooperate with their quest for atonement, the dead will leave us to breathe in peace."

"I'd better be going before the sun dies on me," Senhor Mário Mateus said as he hurried away into the hills.

Perched on the Ginkgo's highest branches, Florindo stared at the hillside across Vale D'Água Amargurada. The hill had been continuously carved into terraces for village crops.

Florindo leaned on the trunk of the Ginkgo, cupped his ear against the bark and listened to the moan of forests, near and distant.

"Dear Ginkgo, what can we do to appease the trees? Ti Clemente and the others don't listen to us!" He stared at the decimated hillside.

Florindo believed the world's knowledge entered trees through their leaves and needles and the irrecoverable story of the world was buried in their roots. The trees stored thoughts in their roots. If turned into stumps, they became unable to exhale their memory, unable to release their stories. Scarlet, fallen leaves were cut-off tongues scattered on the ground. Felled tress were lives cut short, denied old age and denied the slow farewell years of passing on their accumulated wisdom to new saplings.

As the hillside forest disappeared, Florindo noticed decay in the village mood. Ti Anastácio, who had never swatted a fly, began kicking his long time canine companion, Peyto, curled at his feet, anytime the nearly deaf creature did not obey his orders to move. Felismina Alves, the village curandeira who for decades had burrowed in the reclusive heart of the south slope, could not cure the simplest cold. She appeared to have forgotten her spells and the whereabouts of her sacred ingredients. Ti Clemente broke agreement after agreement, alleging he did not remember shaking hands on it. People grew obsessively ensnared in the mudslides of the past, forgetting the essence which held fast the soil and grounded the soul in the world.

At the end of a village day, the sky perspired in a blush of burgundy and boys clustered under the Ginkgo tree. They wrung their hands, waiting for advice to quiet the nagging awkwardness of their enamoured hearts.

"Will you make up a lovely poem I can give Rosa?" Armando asked him, a rose bud tucked behind his ear.

"Love is not embedded in words," Florindo said. "To be certain of love's presence, to be certain that you aren't ensnared in the mirage of the eyes, you must kiss." Florindo kneeled to a daisy and drew a deep breath. "Kiss deep, kiss long. Invite Rosa's fervent breath into your lungs. Keep your spirit door open. Your tongues, guardians of spirit, will be silent in their dance. They will commune. Unimaginable feelings will stir and surface, your histories will mingle. You'll be of each other," Florindo paused and nibbled on the white petals. "You'll know truth, the other's innermost secrets. Be delicate with these treasures. No matter how many hills may rise up between you and Rosa, scent and taste will link you forever."

A breath of wind dropped a handful of blonde leaves. They

fell in Florindo's lap. He blushed. Autumn had arrived to undress the Ginkgo. Florindo sat shyly next to his beloved tree.

"Florindo, if you are so in love, why don't you wed your Ginkgo?" Bonifácio Careta asked. He was always eager to play matchmaker and never missed an opportunity to suggest a wedding. Florindo winked at the Ginkgo. He closed his eyes, placed his palm on her trunk.

"Now, that's a sweet idea," Florindo said.

On Sunday, the children hung garlands of violets from the branches. In the ceremony that Padre Lucas refused to bless, there were no words spoken. Felismina Alves tattooed the Ginkgo Biloba's initials on Florindo's arm and he carved his on the tree with his thumbnail. In their beaks, birds ferried blackberries from the riverside bushes and showered the guests. The children lay on their backs, mouths open, tongues ready to snatch the cascading berries.

The Ginkgo's leaves rustled like castanets and Florindo, clicking his heels, swung around her trunk dancing his happiness while Prudêncio Casmurro played the concertina.

The villagers pretended the idea was insane. But sitting on the opposite side of the River Caima, fishing or weaving orange osier twigs into baskets, they followed the merry events.

"I guess you'll move in together onto a tree house," Ti Clemente yelled. The women shooed him, clapping to the concertina. In the din of merriment, his words never crossed the river.

December cold had settled on the valley. Women were busy in their kitchens, baking fruit cakes and soaking salted cod for Christmas Eve. Ti Clemente and bands of villagers, axes on their shoulders, marched into the woods in search of the perfect pine tree. Florindo followed them in silence and lit candle lanterns on the stumps of the fallen trees. At night, next to his Ginkgo, he sang his prayers above the drifting hymns of the church congregation celebrating the birth of their Creator.

Florindo celebrated Christmas by hanging olive oil lanterns from the fingertips of his Ginkgo and spreading white cotton candy over her branches. One by one, after midnight Mass, the children sneaked out of their houses and perched on the Ginkgo, singing and licking the cotton candy. The children in their colourful garments dangling from branches, their scarves swaying in the air, resembled living tree decorations. A bonfire, from the Ginkgo's fallen leaves and branches, roasted Ginkgo seeds. The white kernels, Florindo regarded as a delicacy.

That evening while the adults slept, Florindo and the children passed through the translucent night planting seeds on the periphery of the village. They planted and sang, "Dance wind dance, waltz a seed, you must believe, trees will live."

Year after year, unnoticed by the villagers, trees regenerated around the village, forming a solid protective shield of greenery.

Village men gathered around the transistor radio at Ti Anastácio's *adega* listening to the evening news while Florindo nestled in his Ginkgo listening to the wind. He sat motionless, eyes closed, letting his belly, his fingers, his toes, fill with air.

Florindo felt the stirrings in the air as the tingle of adverse news gained momentum on the wind. His fingers pulsed. Florindo listened. The villagers turned up the radio, turning a deaf ear to the subtle stirring in their spirits.

Florindo could see the skies darkening to the west. The trees swayed in the wind, rattling their leaves as clouds of dust hovered in the air.

The children curled up like leaves beneath the great Ginkgo. To ease the children's fear, Florindo assured that the enraged winds would not touch them. "They will not harm a cluster of their own," Florindo whispered gravely, pointing to the shield of trees around the village.

Through the night, the Ginkgo trembled and creaked in the

iron wind that was ploughing over the land, sending cattle spinning in the air like pebbles. The Ginkgo stood her ground, and Florindo and the children slept snugly around the tree's feet.

Florindo awoke to the hymns of the church congregation floating across the river.

The hurricane that had swept over the countryside had miraculously left the village relatively unscathed. The villagers marvelled at their Divine fortune. They promised to pray more fervently and to be faithful to the Ten Commandments. Then, in praise to God for sparing their lives and land, they swung axes over their shoulders and marched out to fell the oldest and strongest trees to erect a chapel in honour of the Lord of Heavenly Winds.

Vera

Vera rested, curled in the shade of the womb, meditating on the journey ahead, inch by inch building strength and filling with readiness; readiness, invisible as air that inflates lungs and lends might to voice, invisible as wind that sculpts landscapes and lends shape to the world. Vera rested until the sting of the syringe ejected her out of her dormant state. She sprang forward, initiating the contractions that flushed her towards the sliver of light and into the blur of expectant faces. Vera darted into the world wearing a premature coat of long black hairs which prompted her brother to scream in delight on first seeing her, "A little monkey!!!"

Such disturbance, timely orchestrated, to please and greet her father, returning that weekend from several months absence in a bloody military incursion in the southern hemisphere. "Demonstrating to insubordinate rebels the rules of civility and democratic behaviour," he proclaimed at the end of his speech in the town square. Nothing could be more festive to welcome the hero home than a living monument to his flesh and blood.

In the cradle Vera cried incessantly. Her parents blamed the summer heat and the curse of flies. They drew the blinds, sentencing the house to darkness. Vera's cries persisted. Her parents concluded boredom to be the culprit and buried Vera in plush bears. The bears could not brighten up her life. Vera feared the absence of light. In darkness she lost the colour and the contour of her world. The brass post of her cradle rose out of the dimness above her infant eyes in the shape of a giant needle.

Her brother, now disappointed at Vera's inability to swing from trees, blew into her gasping mouth, temporarily choking her into silence. "Stop crying and you'll be happy," he screamed in exasperation. Vera's cries intensified. She tightened her fists and sunk her nails into her flesh, blood filling the carved-out grooves.

Guiltily, her brother surrendered to her cries. He leaned over the cradle and rested his head next to her body, safely anchoring the flailing distressed hand onto his ear. Vera held onto the ear, a shipwrecked sailor clinging to life. She rubbed his earlobe between her thumb and forefinger and her hiccuping breaths subsided. With a fold of the bed sheet, her brother dried the mixture of tears and perspiration that soaked her hair and urged blood to her cheeks. He pulled the string on the musical chime,

> "Rock a bye baby
> on the tree top
> when the wind blows
> the cradle will rock."

Vera fell asleep from exhaustion and her brother slowly pulled away. Sensing abandonment, Vera woke screaming. Over time, her brother learned to leave a pig's ear in her hand.

As Vera grew older she followed her mother from chore to chore, clinging to her apron, never willing to rest far from the comfort of an overflowing breast. At afternoon tea, Vera steered her mother to the window-seat where she climbed onto her lap to spy, through laced curtains and clouds of flies, children running colourful kites across the public square. Vera would never have parted with the warmth of her mother's bosom had it not been for her father. In a fit of jealousy, he yanked her from the maternal fountain saying, "Time for adult fare." Squeezing her cheeks together, he loaded down her throat a bowlful of pumpkin soup. As the last spoonful disappeared into her mouth, and before her father found time to congratulate himself on the success of his mission, jets of pumpkin mush returned to refill the bowl.

A man of military principles, her father was not to be defeated by anyone's insolence, much less that of a mere child. Between tears and screams he locked into a battle of wills, prying Vera's mouth open to force feed her the pumpkin vomit.

When the time for school arrived, Vera sobbed and pulled on her mother's skirt, pleading for mercy. Sitting next to Vera in the classroom, her mother cramped into a child's desk, bruising her knees. She guided Vera's hand through the twirls of calligraphy and explained, as best she could, "The "b" is really a "d" seen in a mirror, honey. And the "p" is a "b" drying up-side down from a clothes line."

The teacher summoned Vera to the menacing blackboard. The expectant class waited for Vera to write a "d." Without her mother's hand to guide the chalk in her hand, Vera was paralysed under the riotous laughter of fifty children. Panic trickled down her legs, collecting in a puddle of embarrassment. Her mother ran home choking in tears, followed by her sobbing child.

On Sundays, after Mass, valley families gathered on the shores of the River Caima. They hauled baskets overflowing with breads, homemade wines, deep fried pork and, to cut the grease, salted olives. Fathers assembled fishing lines and sat basking in the sunshine. Mothers fanned fires and flies, hurried logs to coals in anticipation of a plentiful catch. Older folk, men and women alike, gathered osier twigs growing in small orange clumps by the river's edge. With bundles under their arms, they returned to sit by the fires where they wove and talked, talked and wove. The dialogue between fingers and voice was an essential part of bringing a basket to life.

Children ventured into the river flapping their skinny limbs, while in the undercurrent, trout flapped scaly fins upstream, to escape the turbulence of Sunday afternoons. Parents indulged their children's attention with competitions for the loudest cannonball plunge, bringing wild laughter from everyone. Vera contented herself flicking stones from shore. Her eyes followed the rings of water, spreading wide, eventually joining the swimming children. On braver days, she allowed the swish of shore water to cover her ankles and pretended to be a water spider. Her long acrobatic legs skimmed the surface of the river, gliding past the other children. From shore she spied her brother, like Tarzan, swinging wildly from a worn out tractor tire suspended from an ancient oak. His splashes aimed at drenching Vera.

One Sunday, Vera's father, enraged by the reflection of his daughter's meekness on himself, tossed her under his arm like a bundle of osier twigs. He marched up the terraces of corn to the stone bridge and dumped her into the current, yelling, "Survival teaches best!"

Vera's petrified body, clenched as a stone, punched the surface of the river, and she sank into the dark water, a familiar darkness numbing her flesh. Her feet hit the sandy bottom and she bounced, swept back towards the light. She surfaced to the blur of expectant faces. Vera's arms flapped, maintaining her head above water until her brother arrived and towed her to shore.

On Sunday evenings there was the usual visit to uncle Virgilio. He owned a dog, much like himself. Xancas did not bark until he was under her behind, the first and last warning before his jaws snapped. Vera's jaws clenched, she did not scream. She dropped none of the apples she was carrying in her apron because uncle Virgilio was notorious for his bad tempers, especially when the apples were bruised. One Sunday, Vera placed one apple after another on the grass, and dropping on all fours, growled at Xancas before lunging in the air and sinking her teeth into the dog's scruff. This bravery was lost to the stars. There were no witnesses applauding Vera's defiant act and encouraging her to tackle the world.

When Vera came of age, her father enlisted his military strategies to secure her a husband.

On the pretence of showing off the bucolic beauty of the region, he brought home young, promising officers soon departing overseas. He pointed to springs cascading down ravines, he exalted the crystalline water reflecting the luxuriant greenery of the grasses, leaves and mosses. "Verdant and fecund," he said. "Turns you green with envy, oh la la."

For dinner he presented the young officers with delicacies from the valley, shepherd cheese and green wine. "Green wine," they exclaimed doubtful. "A cast of wine unique to our region," Vera's father reassured, "Demands less patience than a Burgundy. Burgundy requires excessive aging and maturing in dark cellars." They nodded and he continued. "These grapes are picked green, low alcohol. Extremely safe." The young officers brought the goblet to their lips, drank, gazing at Vera and enjoying the unexpectedly light tingle on their tongues.

VERA

At first it sounded like the roar of a distant storm. Then it sounded like the end of the world. The drone of engines brushed the roof of her home. The stone walls trembled. Vera hurried out in time to see his hand waving and a twirling daisy carried away by a gust of wind. He flew a courting circle on polished wings of silver, displaying the red and green colours of the nation, and departed with a dramatic pirouette into the sunset. How could she say no to her brother's best friend, a man of such pleasant manners, going to such trouble to impress her? After the deafening roar dissipated, she opened the envelope tied to a loaf of bread in the courtyard, "Leaving for Africa, today. Marry me by proxy." Vera fainted. What could she say after the town's people came out to applaud, envying her luck, and her father's nod of approval, "The military has never produced anything but the highest character." Her father's proud, bulging chest was living proof of the fact.

Vera was towed down the aisle, her arm locked in her father's. Her father would not be stepping aside halfway to the pulpit, there would be no groom snapping her father's arm lock. The groom was sun tanning on the West Coast of Africa. Vera reminded herself it was just fine, the Pope had signed the rolled manuscript she held tightly in her free hand. She tried to paste her future husband's grin onto her father's face, but she had forgotten what he looked like and she could not shake the reality that it would be her father's voice that would say, "I do."

Vera paused partway down the aisle. The church bells tolled and the pipe organ lured her to the altar. Her eyes followed the crisscross path of a fly running across her veil. She heard the buzz of other flies around her ears.

Vera remembered her childlike hand attempting to capture the buzzing creatures feasting on the kitchen table crumbs.

Nothing eluded the flies' watchful rotating eyes as they escaped to the windowsill rubbing their legs, mocking Vera's efforts. In despair, Vera would run outside and hide in the neighbour's kennel. One day she fell asleep and failed to notice Bruno, the enormous St. Bernard galloping in her direction. Vera found herself trapped inside the dog's house choking in a mantle of dog hair. A crowd of two bodies. She screamed. It echoed inside Vera's skull, never finding a way out through the maze of hairs that filled her throat.

The church bells stopped, and the pipe organ's notes were suspended in the air. Vera stood paralysed, halfway to the altar. The buzz of voices whispering in the pews crescendoed. With a quick swish of her hand Vera caught the fly criss-crossing her veil. Trapping the fly between her thumb and ring finger she plucked first one wing, then the other. The fly hopped on the palm of her hand. Vera wondered what sort of a life the fly could expect now.

In the midst of her musings, Vera's father pinched her arm. The stinging pain propelled Vera down the aisle, past the blurred crowd of expectant faces, to Father Lucas and the pair of gold rings that waited for her.

Birthing Stones

Along cornfields, past woods, across creeks, Francisco led the villagers to the birthing stones. Large boulders, christened by him as the mothers, covered the crest of the ridge on the rocky landscape of Serra da Senhora da Freita.

The Sunday excitement was so high that Mass was prayed on the trail while the rosary of people following Francisco trekked beneath dawn's first rays. The villagers could have been his goats, but for the prayers echoing against the rising escarpment. Prayers far louder than the tinkle of livestock bells.

Francisco had been criss-crossing the range since he was a child. First, accompanying his cousins and the herds of sheep, later, on his own with his goats.

In the height of summer, he climbed the top ridges. Ridges as familiar as the knuckles on his hand. He filled his shepherding days playing his fife, imitating the wind, the black birds and any creature that caught his fancy. At night he joined his herd in their wild beds of furze, tucking between the furry bodies to sleep.

"The mother-stones have been giving birth, pushing small stones out of their wombs, since the beginning of time," Francisco informed the stupefied villagers who clustered around him. "You are standing in the birth place of the world."

The villagers stared at the small iridescent stones cradled like oysters in the pouch-like notches of mother-stones. Once the men, women and children had satisfied their first curiosity, and being tired and hungry from the long trek, they dispersed for lunch. Florindo Ramos and the more reverent villagers, fearing the powers in the mighty stones, picnicked further away on the meadow, an olive stone's spit from the creek. Ti Clemente and the more adventurous placed blankets over the boulders, improvising tables for curd cheese, corn bread and wine.

After the meal, the children, attracted by the stones' layers of sediment that resembled golden scales, rushed to collect the oyster-shaped babies. On the laps of the mother-stones the children saw indentations, pouch-like notches where the birthed stones had leaped to life. Puzzled, they tried to return the newborn stones to the their mother's arms. The young were enthralled in this task until they were dragged away in tears when the sun faded that evening.

Francisco played his fife, leaning on a mother-stone, one foot tapping. He smiled at his dog busily swinging its tail to the melody. Through the corner of his eye he watched the men distance themselves from the children's racket, meandering towards other outcrops of stones. They paced, hands in their pockets, curiously kicking at the boulders. Correia poked around with his stethoscope trying to hurry the birthing process, "Needs that extra little push, I can tell," Correia said, returning the stethoscope to his pocket. Animated discussions followed. The men waited anxiously for stones to leap from the wombs. They dreamed of catching them in mid-flight, "Better luck if they don't touch the ground," Mayor Ressaca voiced. Slowly, Ti Clarissa and the other women, tired of the young treading on their heels, trickled into the men's company and observed, arms crossed over bosoms.

"Leave them in peace. They've survived without your help for all these years," said Ti Clarissa, grimacing at Ti Clemente, her husband. The men ignored her. She slid her hand, caressing ever so lightly the contour of a baby stone's head. She picked up one stone and held it to her chest.

Ti Clemente, rubbing his callused hands together, gathered courage and climbed onto the top of a mother-stone. A long whistle of awe was heard. Other men joined him.

From atop the mother-stone, the view reached over mountain ranges. For an instant, the men believed they could touch the ocean of Hell's Mouth Bay to the west, and Viseu to the east. Both a day's distance on foot.

"It's true when they say the desire of the eye travels faster than the desire of a heart. A heart must pull flesh, bone, a complete body along," said Professor Manecas, and all nodded in agreement.

"It's a peek of heaven up here. What a view to be born with!" Padre Lucas pronounced, lifting the cross on his chest and offering a panoramic blessing.

"Nothing ordinary here," concurred Correia, placing a hand on Padre Lucas' shoulder.

"Lucky stones. Not like ourselves, born in the pit of the valley where fog and rain slice through our bones. We have to climb uphill to get anywhere," complained Ti Clemente, spitting a mouthful of tobacco.

"Sacred places are always sunnier," Padre Lucas reminded.

Everyone nodded in assent.

"These lucky ones," Mayor Ressaca spoke, pointing at the birthing stone under his feet, "born with a golden view. They only have to roll over themselves and tumble their way down the hill and into the stream where they travel places and populate the world."

"Born in golden cradles," concluded Ti Clemente.

The lowering sun bloodied the crest of the hill. Francisco shielded his eyes and drew a sip of water from the gourd, keeping a curious ear on the conversation.

Ferreira, watching glittering sparks reflecting the sunshine, reasoned the baby stones must contain gold seeds, "All riches of the earth must be trapped in the entrails of the small rocks." "Certainly closer to God up here," Padre Lucas insisted. The Padre's words were lost in the excitement. The villagers huddled closer to Ferreira, not to miss a single word. Quim, distracted by the hares hopping across the meadow, and dreaming of rising pelt prices, pricked his ears up at the mention of gold.

"If it's true that these rocks are the seeds of the world, and if it's true the universe has started in this place, it follows that the world's riches must be contained in my hand," Quim, concluded. He tossed a baby stone up into the air. "I'll pack up some," he added. This stirred a wave of consternation from the more reverent town folk.

But it was not long before they grew accustomed to the idea and Ti Clemente suggested, "Let us take the baby stones to the village and plant them in a field. We'll harvest a ripe crop of gold!" Ti Clemente cheered. He welcomed the prospect of divine providence releasing him from the back-breaking hoe.

"In this time of fortune, remember the dear Lord who has never let us down," Padre Lucas called out.

The villagers swore to secrecy and gathered up their belongings stuffing each pocket with a stone.

Having spent the day staring at the swollen mother-stones, they left without the good fortune of witnessing one miraculous birth.

"Shy stones," said Ti Clarissa, casting a last glance at the boulders. "I don't blame them, a whole town staring down at their bellies," she added, walking away.

Sitting on the ridge above the village with his goats, Francisco could see that the baby stones were not living up to expectation. Weeds proliferated, but otherwise, the fields were indifferent to the rocky seeds. The villagers, wishing not to disturb the stones from their golden task and the promised bounty of riches, watched their crops struggle. They remembered Quim's words, "Money germinates in the smarts of one's head," and grew uneasy.

Word spread that it would require excessive waiting for the stones to mature, produce anything worth their weight.

"After all, the world was not created in one day," reminded Padre Lucas. There was a ring of sensibility in the familiar words.

Winter was at the door and the grain cellars were not filled. Quim gathered the villagers in the town square. "We need to bring a mother-stone down here to get the trapped riches out of her," he asserted. Then they would reap a harvest of gold. Every able body was conscripted to help bring down a birthing stone.

And again the villagers followed Francisco up the hill.

The first birthing stone was rolled down the slope in the belief that this technique required the least effort. But they witnessed the enormous stone disappear into the ravine and crash with a blast. Francisco's goats scattered. He and his dog spent the rest of the day gathering his herd while the discouraged villagers returned home. Quim suggested moving the village to the top of the ridge. Ti Clemente and other elders firmly refused, rooting their arguments and stubborn feet in the ground of the valley's history. Gil and some other youths, restless for a change of airs, packed their traps and moved further up the mountain side.

Francisco continued to shepherd his herd to the pastures while the villagers argued over the gains and the losses of relocation. Word leaked into the neighbouring villages. The secrecy of words could not be contained, needing to give birth to news, wanting to share the loneliness of the discovery. People from Hell's Mouth

Bay and Viseu arrived. And later, strangers from days and day'
journeys appeared wanting to see the stones for themselves. Most
pocketed a tangible memory of their pilgrimage.
Francisco had enjoyed the first curious travellers. Their tales
from faraway brought him new words, other lives. But the occasional traveller had quickly thickened into a stream of excursions,
drowning his silence. More and more people demanded story
upon story of the birthing stones' discovery, "If I don't take a little remembrance my folks will doubt I've stood where the world
first began," pilgrims justified. The saddened guardian of the
treasure, watched and fell silent.

A reporter arrived to set up camp among Francisco's herd. He
conducted interviews and probed for extraordinary stories while
the world dangled by a thin thread of curiosity. Encouraged to
reveal the absurd, villagers and pilgrims competed for the black
and white of their glorious faces dressing the morning front page,
declaring witness to every manner of miraculous events.

"I'll be damned if I wasn't running the tips of my fingers
over the womb of a boulder when it suddenly squirted a stone
into my eye," Ti António, from Hell's Mouth Bay, patch over his
eye, proclaimed. He had regained vision in the opposite eye, he
said, and promised to return annually to honour the birthing
stones' healing abilities.

Padre Lucas swore by his Christian faith that stones were
born at the peak of the day when the sun shone hottest. The
mother-stone exploded from the unbearable heat. Ti Clarissa
swore on her in-laws' graves the stones were never born in the
heat of the day but slid out imperceptibly, without fanfare, under
the concealing blanket of night.

Two men in white coats arrived to scribble notes, measure
angles. They spoke of biotite nodules embedded in granite, flat-
tened billions of years ago. They explained lithological cycles

although few people listened and even fewer mustered the effort to understand their revelations.

The stones' divine characteristics included remedies for diverse afflictions. Helped by those of a religious nature, Padre Lucas erected a chapel around a crop of mother-stones. The huge boulders served as natural altars where continuous candles illuminated the pilgrim's hopes. Their optimistic faith was ablaze with miraculous accounts of the power of the stones. On their knees, people prayed for divine grace to touch them next, believing it simply a question of time and perseverance before their prayers would be answered. The world carried a long line-up of supplications.

The demand for the stones multiplied. Roads were opened to accommodate the traffic and taverns were raised to feed the hungry. The village grew into a thin line that stretched along the roads to the top of the range. Dynamite explosions blasted the peace of the hills. Francisco's tranquillity disappeared. His fife's sound was lost in the thunder of the explosions. Even Sunday's silence, no longer sacred, was pierced by chisels on stone. The weekend masons were poor, but not willing to lose out in the race for a sizeable souvenir. Senhor Mário and other Senhores ordered carved mother-stones. Their mansions became fashionably embellished with the talisman of prosperity.

Francisco's jittery herd dwindled, sacrificed to the claws of traffic. The goats, increasingly suicidal, climbed the highest ridges, jumped off cliffs. Francisco counted more goats lost to the commotion on the hill than in three generations of wolve' hunting for survival.

Francisco moved his livestock farther away to find pastures. The scarce green patches between the criss-cross of the cobblestone roads had been trampled. He knew the miraculous stones would never fill up his goats' bellies, satiate their hunger.

The crowding on the hill brought escalating clashes. Padre Lucas and the firm believers in the holiness of the ridge accused Quim and the miners of greedily raping the site for its riches. The miners swearing on the bible, and also on their picks, announced that the earth was given by God to be partaken of its hidden riches. The two men in white coats accused both parties of destroying the evidence that one day might answer the mysteries of the world.

An election nearing and a pressing deficit stemming from his self-generous compensations, Mayor Ressaca stepped in to referee the angry factions. He surveyed the ridge, listened with special attention to those who donated the fattest pigs and the strongest wine, and decided that all the claims were legitimate and settled the dispute fairly. Every faction received a proportional share of the stones and everyone paid increased taxes.

Mayor Ressaca's decision resolved the conflict until the miners exhausted their share of the hill and looked enviously at the scientists' birthing stones reposing lazily on public lands. Angry, the miners marched to the mayor's office demanding justice, shouting for equality, the right to work and to earn a living. Swinging picks was all they knew how to do. They brandished the picks their grandfathers had used to build the nation.

"They are just stones, for *pits* sake," Quim, their leader shouted. It was unfair, Quim contended, that two men in white coats and a troop of pilgrims hoarded a resource that belonged to the whole country. The miners' labour brought far more wealth than those white coats. They were a blatant national burden, supported by miner's tax-sweated-money. And for what? The dubious purpose of staring at the rocks, elaborating conjectures in indecipherable words.

Mayor Ressaca, another election mandate looming, listened attentively. He graciously accepted the pigs and wine and, reasoning democratic equality, re-divided the remaining mother-stones proportionally.

On a mountain range in the interior, Francisco rested at dusk, contemplating the new electrified home of the birthing stones. As darkness fell, the distant ridge exploded into a fire of light. Francisco feared it would blaze the mountain down to charcoal. The glare obliterated the brightest stars. His dog howled, confused by the intense glow. Francisco decided to investigate the state of the world's cradle.

In the new town, Francisco peered into a shop displaying miniature carved miners pushing wheelbarrows loaded with baby stones. The next window offered carvings mounted on velvet stands. Another featured gigantic rosaries beaded from baby stones. Every shop had identical postcards picturing the pristine ridge of an earlier time. Memories for sale, Francisco told his dog and goats, following him on the sidewalk.

Francisco meandered past a tavern reeking of vomit. He recognised Quim shooing out Manecas, the last customer, before slamming the door in his drunken face. He crossed paths with Ti Clemente, pushing a mountain of detritus, his downcast eyes planted on the rolling garbage. There were no hares sprinting on what used to be a meadow. Instead, a scurry of rats was diving into the gutters chased by mongrel dogs. The magpies slept, perched on dumpsters. Francisco's goats were attracted to the salty and greasy trash and refused to move on. He whistled his dog to round up the goats and to lead them onwards.

He walked up the new paved road leading to the ridge. He jumped the iron gate. His goats followed. A foot worn path led them to where the last mother-stone was incarcerated in glass, protected from probing hands.

Francisco worried the world would cease to grow and to renew itself. He wondered how long it would be before the mountain, the world, crumbled of old age and the forgotten birthing stones would germinate once again.

Francisco fell asleep against the glass case of the last mother-stone. He dreamed that the undermined mountain, bone-weakened, folded on its knees and collapsed. A deafening rumble buried everything in a clean sweep while, perched on the very top, he rode it downhill with his anxious goats on his lap.

Ripeness

Prudêncio Casmurro was no ordinary man. He had buried his parents, seven wives and the last of his twenty-two children, and showed no readiness to depart the mortal world.
He had seen ox-pulled wooden carts replaced by tractors and tractors replaced by combines. From his bedroom window he peered over his walled garden at the world whirling faster and faster, screeching louder and louder, shining brighter and brighter, making it difficult for Prudêncio to distinguish between night and day. Donkey-stubborn, he continued on with his life. Those were passing winds outside his window, and he simply drew his curtains.

Prudêncio woke with the first rays of morning and strolled to his front porch to stretch his arms to the rain or the sun, whichever one was ruling. He greeted either with the same jovial whistle and exclamation, "Another splendid day in our valley!" Wearing his nightgown and toque, he walked barefoot to the garden and plucked fruit in season. Persimmons in the chill of winter, cherries in the blush of spring.

Prudêncio chewed every bite and leisurely savoured the fruit cultivated in his fragrant soil. After each mouthful he paused, thoughtful, honouring the visible and invisible which had brought the sustenance into his body. His head nodded, bowing to the world, before he proceeded to the next mouthful.

He ate nothing not ripened in the soil of his garden, except at his great-grandchildren's weddings, where he indulged in Fuji apples and Appalusian beans cultivated by trusted hands. While sitting on his stone veranda chewing his food, Prudêncio listened to the canto of the blackbirds and followed the buzz of the bumblebees at work in his camomile patch. Prudêncio kept no animals. He preferred spirited beings arriving and departing with independent will and planted dandelions and milkweed on the edge of the garden to attract butterflies. He dug a pond where frogs made their home and mallards returned to nest, generation after generation. Prudêncio cherished simple moments in his garden—a butterfly landing on his chest, wings opening and closing in syncopation with his heart beat, a frog leaping from the bottom of the porch stairs into his lap.

Prudêncio was not a superstitious man, but there was one matter in his world for which he had no tolerance—clocks. Prudêncio was born when clocks were the size of coffins, standing in prominent display. A golden pendulum swung back and forth in their bellies. It mesmerised the gathering of neighbours.

Not to be outdone by Ti Celestino up the road, Prudêncio's father had carried home his proud purchase on his back. His father placed the clock on top of the stairs, against Prudêncio's bedroom wall. The clock's strident bell echoed hourly inside Prudêncio's skull, shattering his dreams, shuddering his bones. Every night, Prudêncio rose from bed and silenced the pendulum. But next morning, his father had the pendulum in full swing again. Finally one night, Prudêncio tossed the winding key into the well. Already perplexed by the continuous morning quiet, and then finding the key missing, his father believed the clock was haunted. He threw his arms in the air, giving up on the cursed tool. The clock rested in a dim corner of the house for the remainder of Prudêncio's childhood, silenced at one minute to midnight. "I'm going to follow the cycles of nature. No crazy human invention to measure time will suit me," Prudêncio vowed.

He had been told that, with the passing decades, clocks had shrunk so small a person could thread one through a needle's eye. "Those time-stealers proliferate faster than rats, stealing the cheese of our existence," Prudêncio fumed when informed that there was no object which did not display time—month and year —and that most people even tied clocks to their wrists. Prudêncio shook his head. He could not understand why anyone would willingly handcuff themselves to time.

"Don't be stubborn Dad," Gil, his eldest child, had cajoled him. "Change is the human constant. Adapting to change is our survival. Ask Darwin. You'll be going down the dinosaur road."

Prudêncio's son died in his thirties. Mesmerised by electronic gadgets, he brought his collection of electronic decorations to his grave as if he belonged to an exotic tribe. Television, telephone, watch-pen, walkman. Sundays, after the Casmurro children had obediently attended church—Prudêncio had stopped attending Mass the day the priest placed a clock in the steeple—Gil liked to hop on a bus to the city and meander through the streets, window shopping for electronic novelties. Gil dreamed of the gadgets he would give himself on his next birthday. He hid them at a neighbour's house. No time keeping devices were permitted inside Gil father's stone walls.

Prudêncio refused to celebrate birthdays. "If you don't know how old you are, your body will never know when it's time to quit. I'll just circle around and around with the seasons."

None of his late twenty-two children or his surviving thirteen great-grandchildren had convinced him to attend a birthday party—theirs or his. "A principle is a principle. If you aren't going to stand for principles—and for people of course—what else would you stand for?"

His great-grandchildren speculated that Prudêncio Casmurro had been around anywhere from two to three centuries. His turnip-coloured beard dangled to his knees, and his hair spiralled like a garlic braid to his ankles. He declined medical examinations, refused marketers promoting facial creams that claimed to erase years or supplements to boost the body's stamina. "Tending a garden, bending to weeds, lifting and carrying baskets, builds the stamina your body needs."

Prudêncio Casmurro became a tourist attraction. "The oldest man alive lives here," a banner proclaimed. Busloads of tourists stopped at his walls, snapped an obligatory picture of the quaint and colourful graffiti, "Jesus Lives Here," and "Snakes and Apples, too," then departed hastily for the next stop at the papermill. Expensive tours, in helicopters, circled Prudêncio's roof attempting to photograph his illusive presence below.

As predictable as nature's cycles, Prudêncio could count on seasons of resentment from his village, now sprawled into a metropolis. Gossip of his pacts with the devil abounded to explain his longevity. With the passing of time and the isolation, he had no one to share his memories. Old friends had long passed on, leaving him to carry the stories, the remembrances. On hot summer nights, he picked his concertina and turned their life stories into music, singing to the chorus of frogs croaking beneath grapevines. Prudêncio missed his grandparents sitting by the loom, weaving yarns from a time before him, a time pregnant with mystery and questions.

It had been an eternity since Prudêncio had had a wife. He felt more and more estranged from the world and saw less and less of his dying great-grandchildren, every one too old now to visit him on their own and dwelling in high rises where no one could exit without help or permission.

His garden remained his only love. The garden rooted him to the world, still needing his hands, his touch, to live on.

Prudêncio came to recognise that he could not avoid the piercing arrow of time outside his walls, the inexorable movement of people and their desires. The urban roar screeched louder than a mad beast's wail. The city bulged. Glass buildings shot skyward and stared down at him, closing in like predators. He no longer felt at ease soaking in his wooden tub amid his strawberry patches, scrubbing his back, reaching for a berry in sunshine. The patch of blue above him shrunk, and it was no longer blue but perpetually grey. Fewer and fewer birds returned with spring to whistle in the umbrella of his orchard. The stinking deadly winds of the paper mills up the river valley trespassed his walls. The tender cherry trees stopped flowering. The golden plums embellishing the tree's crown showed strange burns on their fair skin, some scarred to the core. The well's water tasted foul. A bothersome cough settled in his chest.

Prudêncio could no longer draw his curtains to the outside world. In the refuge of his bed, jets roaring shook the walls, rattling his mother's crystal collection, crumbling the plaster, jolting him awake. Prudêncio found relief by stuffing cotton balls into his ears, but the wail increased its frequency and intensity. Even burying his head under a pillow brought him no peace. He built himself a cushioned, soundproof box where he found rest from the trepidation and noise of the world. Every night he climbed into his box and closed the lid. His life was shrinking, and Prudêncio, molelike, was burrowing deeper and deeper. He climbed into his coffin at the day's end to find peace and rose in the morning to stare at himself in the mirror—at the wrinkles in his face sinking faster, his eyes losing their shine. A ghost.

Swinging in his hammock, watching a hummingbird flap its wings so hurriedly they appeared still, Prudêncio made a decision. He walked to his gate and unchained his world. To the few passersby who did not flee, he offered freshly harvested strawberries, and invited them inside. Prudêncio showed them the worms and the birds, the pond and the orchard. They listened to gentle wind chimes dangling from the branches, humming in the breeze. After some months of visitors, a few began to linger behind, helping him weed, taking home to their loved ones a peach or a plum. They returned in the evenings to listen to Prudêncio's stories. A world strange as history, peopled with feats, sorrows and dreams.

With the first rays of morning, children knocked on his door and filled his garden with games of hide-and-seek and hopscotch. Bird nests and tree houses nestled in the orchard branches. Painters set up their easels and sketched bees at work in the camomile flowers.

The garden thrived. There was never shortage of help. On weekends people brought picnics and ate under the fruit trees. Voices in song flourished above the city roar and Prudêncio never again sang alone.

Throughout the city, pots of flowers began to smile from windowsills. Sprinkles of green appeared in sidewalk cracks and cement was torn up to give room to small garden plots. A sweeter scent infiltrated the city air.

On an unusually starry night, Prudêncio voiced goodnights to a group of his faithful visitors spending a fortnight in his orchard studying bats feasting on apricots. He laid in his hammock, dangling between a lemon and a peach tree. Prudêncio inspected his garden, listened to the rhythmical swish of bat wings scooping up clouds of insects; frenzied insects celebrating the end of a busy day pollinating. Prudêncio relished his garden humming so happily now, smiling so colourfully.

An owl scrutinised the ever-changing shadows dancing on the ground. Frogs croaked tirelessly in the background. The garden's bountiful crops nourished innumerable caring hands. His work was complete. Prudêncio closed his eyes and willed himself to leave.

The gentle morning breeze found Prudêncio in his hammock, enveloped in a blanket of butterflies. The butterflies fanned their wings. The hammock swayed. Robins, perched on the hammock's rope, sang. Through the overcast sky, a beam of sunshine wrapped Prudêncio's body in gold. Frogs croaked a solemn requiem. Sunflowers graciously turned their heads and bowed. A white rain of almond petals floated from the sky. The morning had arrived to greet Prudêncio Casmurro before he returned to the earth.

Acknowledgements

The creation of a book does not rest in the hands of a single person, just as the fruit on a tree is not the sole creation of the hands that have tended it. The body of writers, books and words preceding me are the supportive ground, a fertile foundation nourishing and urging the future. There must be water, pollinating wings, and an abundant bacterial life, invisible to our human eye, to bring a book to fruition. My gratitude goes to those named and those unnamed, who in obvious and subtle ways have contributed to the book in your hand. These include the worms, the forest and the logger.

I am indebted to a number of writers who generously gave of their time and whose editorial fine eye helped these stories grow: David Albahari, Darlene Barry, Ven Begamudré, Ashis Gupta, Richard Harrison, Larissa Lai, Shirlee Matheson, George Melnyk, Rosemary Nixon, Peter Oliva, Richard Therrien and D.M. Thomas. I would also like to thank the Markin-Flanagan Distinguished Writers Programme for bringing many of these writers to Calgary and making them accessible to the local writing community for editorial consultation.

Thanks to Jim Prager and Lucy Nissen for the years of editorial endurance. I am particularly indebted to Lucy Nissen for her thorough manuscript edit.

For financial assistance during the writing of this book, I am grateful to the Canada Council for the Arts.

Obrigado to my immediate and extended family of natural storytellers for preserving generations of family stories. Those were the seeds that took flight in the wind of my imagination and eventually became this book.

The story "Ripeness" is for Jim Prager for the timely seed.

A heartfelt thanks to my friends who nurtured and encouraged me on my literary path. There are too many of you to name. You know who you are.

Thank you also to Galen Bullard for the friendship and the eye to detail.

To my publisher Richard Olafson who believed in this manuscript, my thanks.

A sweet thanks to Erin Hart for her unwavering support and generosity, inside and outside the book.

This book is for my friends and family of yesterday, today and tomorrow.

In earlier incarnations and under different titles some of these stories were published or broadcasted by CBC Radio, *The Animist* (Australia), *Southern Ocean Review* (New Zealand), *The Art Bin* (Sweden), *Albedo One* (Ireland), *Writing on Air: MIT Press Anthology* (USA) as well as in Portuguese translation by *Revista Ópio* (Portugal). Under the early title of "Hell's Mouth Bay," the story "The Scent of a Lie" was first published in 2001 by Canongate Books, Edinburgh, in the anthology, *Original Sins: The Canongate Prize for New Writing.*